KT-592-168

THE NEW PROPHECY

Book One: Midnight

Book Two: Moonrise

Book Three: Dawn

Book Four: Starlight

Book Five: Twilight

Book Six: Sunset

POWER OF THREE

Book One: The Sight

Book Two: Dark River

Book Three: Outcast

Book Four: Eclipse

Book Five: Long Shadows

Book Six: Sunrise

OMEN OF THE STARS

Book One: The Fourth Apprentice

Book Two: Fading Echoes

Book Three: Night Whispers

Book Four: Sign of the Moon

Book Five: The Forgotten Warrior

Book Six: The Last Hope

DAWN OF THE CLANS

Book One: The Sun Trail

Book Two: Thunder Rising

Book Three: The First Battle

Book Four: The Blazing Star

Book Five: A Forest Divided

Book Six: Path of Stars

A VISION OF SHADOWS

Book One: The Apprentice's Quest

Book Two: Thunder and Shadow

EXPLORE THE
WARRIORS WORLD

THE GATHERING DARKNESS

SURVIVORS

DEAD OF NIGHT

ERIN
HUNTER

HARPER

An Imprint of HarperCollinsPublishers

Special thanks to Rosie Best

Dead of Night
Copyright © 2016 by Working Partners Limited
Series created by Working Partners Limited
Endpaper art © 2016 by Frank Riccio
All rights reserved. Printed in the United States of America.
No part of this book may be used or reproduced in any manner whatsoever without
written permission except in the case of brief quotations embodied in critical
articles and reviews. For information address HarperCollins Children's Books, a
division of HarperCollins Publishers, 195 Broadway, New York, NY 10007.
www.harpercollinschildrens.com

Library of Congress Control Number: 2015961050
ISBN 978-0-06-234339-0

Typography based on a design by Hilary Zarycky
17 18 19 20 21   OPM   10 9 8 7 6 5 4 3 2 1
❖
First paperback edition, 2017

For Jessie, who sleeps like the dead.

LIGHTHOUSE

HIGH WATCH

WILD PACK CAM

THE ENDLESS LAKE

LONGPAW TOWN

RIVE

PACK LIST

WILD PACK (IN ORDER OF RANK)

ALPHA:

female swift-dog with short gray fur (also known as Sweet)

BETA:

gold-and-white thick-furred male (also known as Lucky)

HUNTERS:

SNAP—small female with tan-and-white fur

BRUNO—large thick-furred brown male Fight Dog with a hard face

BELLA—gold-and-white thick-furred female

MICKEY—sleek black-and-white male Farm Dog

STORM—brown-and-tan female Fierce Dog

ARROW—black-and-tan male Fierce Dog

WHISPER—skinny gray male

WOODY—stocky brown male

PATROL DOGS:

MOON—black-and-white female Farm Dog

TWITCH—tan male chase-dog with black patches and three legs

DART—lean brown-and-white female chase-dog

DAISY—small white-furred female with a brown tail

RAKE—scrawny male with wiry fur and a scarred muzzle

BREEZE—small brown female with large ears and short fur

CHASE—small ginger-furred female

BEETLE—black-and-white shaggy-furred male

THORN—black shaggy-furred female

RUFF—small black female

OMEGA:

small female with long white fur (also known as Sunshine)

PROLOGUE

"A Fierce Dog never hides!" *Grunt* snarled up at the big golden dog, planting his oversized puppy paws firmly in the leaf mulch. Lick's heart pounded fearfully as she watched him. Their other litter-brother, Wiggle, gave a nervous whine and shuffled closer to the black-and-white dog's flank.

Lick knew why Grunt was angry.

Something is coming for us, and the golden dog knows what it is.

The two grown-up dogs had been talking in low growls as they walked, thinking the pups couldn't hear them or smell their growing fear-scent. Lick stared up at the golden dog, Lucky, and shuddered from her ears to her drooping tail. He was a big, brave dog. If *he* was afraid of whatever had made those strange howls in the night, then it must be something very bad.

For a moment Lucky seemed to hesitate, staring at Grunt as if the angry pup was as frightening as the danger that stalked them through the darkness.

"Pups, do what we do," said Mickey, Lucky's black-and-white Packmate. He threw himself to the ground and rolled until his fur was thick with mud and mulch.

Lick rolled too, coating herself until she felt as if she was more mud than pup. Normally she would have enjoyed rolling on the forest floor with her litter-brothers and their new friends, but this was no time for play. She gave little Wiggle an encouraging nudge with her wet nose, helping him to cover himself until his familiar warm, milky smell was lost under the scent of the forest.

"You must resist the urge to wash yourselves," Mickey said, and Wiggle froze, his little pink tongue half out to clean the muck from his coat. "That's good. Now we need to be very quiet and still." Mickey crawled underneath a bush, and Lick and Wiggle followed. Lick's litter-brother burrowed in close to Mickey's side and hid his trembling muzzle in the big dog's fur. Lick wanted to hide her face too, but she couldn't make herself look away. Whatever the monsters were, she had to see them coming.

I wish our Mother-Dog were here. She was big and strong. She would drive the monsters away.

But there was no Mother-Dog in the Garden now, no Pack or

longpaws to look after them. Their Mother-Dog had gone away—to be with the Earth-Dog, Lucky had said—and there was no food and had been no dog to tell them what to do now, until the two strange dogs had arrived.

Lick hoped that the Earth-Dog was taking care of her Mother-Dog. They had buried her body before they left the Garden, along with the cold, still pup they had found lying in the long grass.

Lick's ears pressed themselves down against her skull, and she suppressed the urge to whimper. She could smell the monsters now. For a moment she thought that they were dogs, but this wasn't like the scent that had lingered in the Dog-Garden or the one Mickey and Lucky carried around with them. It was sharper, unfamiliar.

When the pups had left their home, the grown-up dogs had promised to look after them, and Lick had believed them. Now she looked up at Lucky, still standing stiff-legged outside the bush, and hoped the golden-furred dog could keep his promise.

"I'm not hiding from anything," Grunt snarled at Lucky. A tiny growl vibrated in Lick's chest. She wanted to snarl too, and tell her silly litter-brother not to be such a fuzz-head, but she didn't dare draw any more attention.

Grunt turned to walk away, and Lick tensed her haunches,

3

ready to spring out and drag him back to safety by his scruff if she had to. But then she heard the voices, and her courage faltered.

"Where's go cubs?"

"Close, cohorts. Smell cubs . . ."

What are those? Lick thought, horror flattening her belly to the earth.

Lucky lunged forward and shoved Grunt toward the bush. Grunt resisted, his paws scrabbling for a hold in the mud.

Do you have rocks for brains? Lick wanted to howl. *Stop fighting him!*

Finally Grunt slid into the space in the undergrowth beside Lick, and Lucky scrambled in after him, keeping him close. He was muttering something to Grunt that Lick couldn't quite hear, but she heard Grunt's shuddering response. "Coyotes? What are they?"

"I eats the cubs. Starts with the tender snouts!" hissed a rasping voice from nearby.

"I crunch the tails!"

Even Grunt went silent at that, his sides trembling. Lick peered out between the twigs, her eyes wide, and caught a glimpse of shapes moving at the top of the hill. Their outlines were similar to those of dogs, except that their furry bodies were carried on long, thin legs that looked like nothing but skin stretched over bones.

Wiggle burrowed deeper into Mickey's thick fur, and even Grunt squeezed his eyes shut. But Lick refused to look away.

I'm not afraid of going to see the Earth-Dog, she snarled inside her head, as the coyotes came closer and closer. *But no half-dog thing is going to crunch my tail. . . .*

CHAPTER ONE

In the clearing outside the Pack's camp, dogs swarmed around the edges of Storm's vision like panicking shadows, howling and yapping in grief and terror.

The weak paws of the Sun-Dog were brushing the tops of the trees, but they hadn't reached the ground. The light that filtered down to the corpse at Storm's forepaws was gray, matching the ragged fur of the dog's coat.

Only the vivid splashes of blood stood out against the dimness of the dawn.

A dog did this.

Storm sank down to her belly, staring into Whisper's lifeless eyes. His wounds were terrible. No dog could have survived them, let alone sweet, scrawny Whisper. His flank and stomach had been raked with strong claws, and his throat had been torn away.

Storm's paws rested at the edge of a patch of dark earth, almost black, where Whisper had given all his blood to the Earth-Dog.

Storm had seen dead dogs before—lots of them. She remembered their faces. Her Mother-Dog's ears had been flopped forward in sadness. Blade's pup had seemed peaceful, though his death had been anything but. Terror's upper lip had been twisted in a crazed, furious snarl, right to the end.

But Whisper's eyes were wide, his jaw slightly open, as if in surprise.

Who has done this to you?

Storm realized she was panting, shuddering as she breathed. She felt cold, but she didn't know if it was true cold or just the chill of horror.

Her Packmates were still whining and circling Whisper's body. Bruno paced anxiously back and forth, his big paws skittering across the ground, as if he was afraid to touch the earth where Whisper had died. The Pack's Omega, Sunshine, quivered at the foot of a tree, hiding her face behind a clump of grass.

Storm was vaguely aware of some dog howling, "Follow the scent—find them!" A few of the dogs crashed through the bushes and into the trees, little white Daisy and tall, scruffy Rake among them. A moment later they were joined by Mickey, the black-and-white Farm Dog.

It's too late. You can't save Whisper now, Storm thought. *And you won't find his killer. He's been dead too long.* His wounds were drying, and he smelled cold. Whoever had murdered Whisper would be far away by now.

Once again, the thought hit Storm: *A dog did this to Whisper. But which dog?*

"How could this have happened?" Alpha howled, anger overtaking shock in her voice. "This is our territory! Where are the dogs who were on patrol last night?"

"I—I was, Alpha," said Thorn, stepping forward on shaking legs.

"I was leading the patrol, Alpha," said Breeze, coming to Thorn's side. She gave the young dog a reassuring nudge with her nose. Breeze's paws were steady, but when she glanced over at Whisper's body, her brown eyes were deep and dark. "We were running the border of the camp all night. Neither of us saw anything."

It takes a while to get all the way around the camp and back, Storm thought. *It would be easy to avoid the patrol, if a dog didn't want to be seen.* But to know that, the killer must have been watching the Pack and learning the Patrol Dogs' habits . . . and that meant that some dog was out there, a dog they didn't know about, and that dog had chosen to come into their territory to murder poor Whisper.

It didn't make sense.

Unless . . . that dog hadn't needed to pass the patrol at all.

Storm shook her head, as if she could dislodge the thought before it took hold. But it forced its way to the front of her mind despite her efforts. It felt like a betrayal to even consider it, but . . .

What if Whisper's killer had come from within the camp?

Storm glanced around at the other dogs, fearing and hoping at the same time that she wasn't the only one to have thought this. But the rest of the Pack was still focused on Alpha and the Patrol Dogs, who stood with their tails held low.

Alpha glared at Breeze and Thorn, her thin legs trembling with rage and the effort of standing for so long when her belly was swollen with unborn pups. "You didn't see anything. You didn't scent anything. So your patrol failed us."

Dart, Beetle, and Omega all howled in agreement and distress.

"What does this mean?" Omega whined.

Dart dipped her head, and her ears flattened to her skull. "Are our patrols useless?"

"They certainly weren't any use to Whisper," Woody said in a hollow growl.

"The whole point of having Patrol Dogs is to keep danger outside the Pack," Alpha said. She drew herself up to her full height, pricking her ears, and looked down her long nose at Moon and the other Patrol Dogs. "We need better, more frequent patrols. I want twice as many dogs on watch at all times."

Storm's panting breath caught for a moment as all eyes in the Pack turned toward Moon. She was still the lead Patrol Dog, even though Alpha had put her on High Watch as a punishment for the crime of stealing food from the prey pile. A crime Storm was certain Moon had not committed. She must have run down from the cliff at the sound of the dogs' grief. Now she sniffed the air defensively.

"We can double the patrols, Alpha," she said stiffly, "if the Patrol Dogs give up sleeping properly. With the greatest respect," she added, dipping her head in deference to Alpha's glare, "we simply don't have enough dogs, not now that we have scouts going off with the hunters every day. The Patrol Dogs have to rest sometime! Perhaps if I came off High Watch, then—"

"If our enemies do not rest, then neither will we," Alpha snapped. "And you will remain on High Watch until I say otherwise!"

Lucky stepped closer to Alpha, and she leaned against her Beta's golden flank with a grateful sigh. "Alpha is right. We must defend the Pack. And Whisper's death must be avenged," he added. "We have been attacked! We must strike back, and quickly."

Barks of agreement echoed around the clearing as one by one the Pack Dogs' ears pricked up. Bella gave her litter-brother a stern nod. Snap's lips curled back in a snarl, and Woody raked the earth beneath his claws impatiently.

Storm barked a quiet "Yes" along with the rest, but she couldn't summon up any of her Fierce Dog fury right now. Whisper's blank eyes and lifeless paws kept drawing her gaze back, stealing her attention from the Pack's rallying cries.

At least when she looked at Lucky, she felt a small spark of hope.

He has a plan! He must have an idea how we can find out who did this. She sat up attentively, waiting to hear it.

"We know who must have done this," Lucky announced. "Those mangy creatures, the foxes!"

Storm cocked her torn ear, confused. Why would he think that?

"They attacked our camp," Lucky went on, his voice rising into an angry howl. "They believe we killed one of their pups, and this is their revenge! They are insane, evil . . . *not-dogs*! And this time they have gone too far. We will strike back!"

The dogs howled and their tails thudded against the earth in approval.

"Revenge for Whisper!" Breeze said, and Thorn and Beetle both yapped along with her.

"Drive them out of our territory!"

"They'll never hurt a dog again!"

Storm glanced from dog to dog, a whine vibrating in her throat, too quiet for the others to hear. Had any of these dogs actually *looked* at Whisper's wounds? Did Lucky not realize that there was no fox-scent in the clearing?

"That's right! We'll—" Lucky began, then stopped abruptly, his head snapping around to look at his mate. Alpha was nodding along with the Pack's anger, but her legs were trembling, and she blinked slowly, as if she was losing strength, and fast.

"You must get some rest," said Moon, padding over to Alpha, their arguments forgotten. "The pups need you to be still."

"The pups will be fine," said Alpha, but she didn't resist when Beta gently nudged her into a walk, steering her away toward the camp and their den.

Without their Alpha or Beta to lead the discussion, the other dogs had started to gather around Twitch, the Pack's Third Dog, barking over one another in their enthusiasm.

"We'll need to find those fiends' den if we're going to take revenge," said Bruno.

But it wasn't *the foxes. . . .*

Storm pawed the ground anxiously. She had to tell some dog— but she knew that she couldn't simply bound over to the others and contradict what their Beta had just said.

Alpha and Lucky had to be told what had really happened.

She almost couldn't bring herself to leave Whisper. Even his old Packmates had left his side now, turning away to hunt for his killer or join in the talk of revenge. Surely some dog had to stay with him? But it was Storm's duty to tell the two leaders what she'd seen, and so she cast a sad glance back at Whisper and then pushed through the undergrowth, running after them.

It took her only a couple of long strides to reach the edge of the forest and leave the shadows of the trees behind. She ran over the soft, damp grass with the early light of the Sun-Dog gleaming down on her back. The Wind-Dogs carried the faint scent of the Endless Lake over the cliffs to the high, sunlit camp where the Pack had made their home.

Alpha and Lucky weren't moving very fast, hampered by

the swift-dog's tiredness and the extra weight of their pups, and Storm caught up with them as they passed the small pond just outside the camp.

"Alpha! Beta, wait," she barked. With all the dogs out in the forest, the place was eerily quiet, and her bark seemed louder than she'd meant it to. A small bird that had been perched by the edge of the still water startled and flew away. The two older dogs paused.

"What's the matter, Storm? Has something happened?" Lucky asked.

"I—I wanted to talk to you about Whisper."

"Alpha must get some rest." Lucky shook his head. "Can it wait until I get back?"

"I'm all right, Lucky," said Alpha, and gave him an affection- ate nudge with the top of her head. "Why don't you stay and talk to Storm? I can get myself to the den."

"Are you sure?" Lucky said, looking around, as if to search for foxes hiding in the long grass by the pond.

"Are you challenging your Alpha?" his mate teased. "I can walk a few steps by myself. Stay with Storm." She turned her back on him and walked, slowly but with dignity, up the slope toward the den. Lucky kept his eyes fixed on her, watching every step she took until she was out of sight. Storm shifted from paw to paw, feeling a strange prickle of impatience as she waited for her Beta to give her his attention. Her resolve wavered—she suspected he wasn't going to like what she had to say, and it would be so easy to turn around and join the others. . . .

No, I have to tell him!

"I don't think the foxes killed Whisper," Storm blurted out. Lucky's head whipped around, and he fixed her with a wide-eyed stare.

"Of course they did. They believe we killed their pup. That's all the motive they would need. . . ."

"But there was no scent, Lucky! Foxes smell terrible, and there was no scent on Whisper's body except for dogs and . . . and blood."

Lucky's brows drew together, and he stared over Storm's shoulder, back toward the forest, for a long moment. Then he shook his head. "Whisper's body was cold. It must have been there for some time before the patrol stumbled on it—the fox-scents could have faded in that time."

"I don't think so," Storm pressed. "And even if they had, I'm *sure* we would have smelled them in the forest! The patrols didn't report scenting foxes, and I didn't smell any as we came in from the hunt . . . did you?"

Lucky kept on staring toward the forest and didn't answer. Storm guessed he didn't remember—she couldn't blame him for being distracted, when they'd been following the sound of Alpha howling in grief and pain.

"Anyway," she went on, "foxes' jaws are small. Their claws aren't very strong. Come back and look again, and you'll see it too. I think Whisper was killed by a dog."

At that, Lucky's eyes snapped back to focus on Storm. "What? You think the Fierce Dogs did this?" he snarled. Storm's ears pulled back, and she looked away. "Or some other bad dog from outside the Pack?" Lucky added quickly.

Storm didn't meet his eyes. He'd tried to cover it, but Lucky's thoughts had gone straight to her birth Pack, to dogs like her and Arrow.

"I don't know," she said quietly. "I didn't smell any unfamiliar dog scents, but . . ."

Lucky shook his head. "Well, then what dog could have killed him? Storm, I know you're upset, but that's enough." He turned away. "There are no dogs around here who would attack our Pack—we would have met them before. Whisper must have been killed by the foxes."

"But, Beta, the scent—"

"Foxes are cunning creatures," Lucky barked. "They must have covered their scent somehow. And as for the size of their jaws, foxes come in all sizes, just like dogs. That proves nothing."

No, that's not right. I'm sure the bite marks are wrong for a fox. . . . A vision of Whisper's bloodied throat flashed before Storm's eyes. She had to make sure Lucky understood her fear, even if the thought was so dark she could barely allow herself to think it. "Beta," she said again, "what if some dog in our Pack—"

"Quiet, pup!" Lucky's eyes flashed angrily, and Storm shifted back on her paws. "Stop this nonsense, right now. I know it's hard to see something like this happen to a good dog like Whisper. It's hard for the whole Pack. That's why I need you to promise me you won't go bothering the other dogs with this . . . this ridiculous theory!"

Less ridiculous than pinning it on the foxes, Storm thought. *Whether you can face it or not.* But she kept quiet, her head low, as Lucky paced back and forth in front of her, scattering the dew drops with his swishing tail.

"The Pack is under attack, Storm, do you understand that?" Lucky barked. "We need to be strong right now—for Alpha, and the pups, and for every dog. If you start accusing Pack Dogs of murdering one of our own, there will be panic, and they'll turn on each other. They'll turn on *you*, most likely!" Lucky's voice became softer, but no less certain. "The foxes killed Whisper, Storm. I won't hear another word about it."

Without even waiting for Storm to reply, he turned and hurried after Alpha toward their den.

Storm stared after him, unease forming a hot ball in her stomach.

What do I do now?

Her Beta had given her an order—to keep her observations to herself. She shook her coat briskly from head to tail and turned back to the forest, her mind racing, covering rabbit-chases with every step.

He was her Beta, and he didn't just give orders like that on a whim. He *must* have a good reason to believe that the foxes were responsible. Perhaps he knew something she didn't. After all, what was a Pack worth if they couldn't trust their leaders to give orders that made sense?

She broke back into the clearing and her eyes fell on Whisper's body, still lying where he had died. Seeing his wounds again gave her a jolt, as if the Earth-Dog had growled under her feet. With the evidence in front of her, she couldn't deny the truth, even if Lucky had told her to keep it to herself. She was certain foxes could not have done this.

The other dogs were still gathered around Twitch, discussing how they were going to strike back against the fox pack.

"We'll see how those mangy brutes like being attacked in their own camp," Bruno snarled.

Snap bared her sharp fangs. "We should go at night, when they won't be expecting it."

Storm shuddered, but her Beta's order still rang in her ears, and she kept her mouth shut.

She padded over and sat down beside Whisper.

"I'm sorry I left you," she whined.

She knew that if Whisper were alive, he would forgive her nearly anything. She gazed at his torn flank, the fur along her back prickling with shame. All he had ever shown her was kindness and admiration, and how had it made her feel? Embarrassed. Annoyed.

She'd wanted him to leave her alone.

I guess I got my wish, she thought, and bit back a howl of grief and guilt.

Perhaps this was the work of a strange dog, or some creature they'd never seen before. If she could find some other clue to what had killed him and prove that it came from outside the Pack, maybe Lucky would be more willing to listen, and Whisper would be avenged after all.

There had to be *something*. She looked around, trying to sense anything in the clearing that was out of place. At first she saw nothing strange, but as she got to her paws and walked slowly around the edge of the dark stain on the earth, something caught her eye. A trail of grass that lay flat, as if it had been trampled down, leading from Whisper's body into the trees.

No, she realized, looking more closely at the way the blades of grass were lying. *It leads here, from the trees.* It was as if Whisper had been dragged into the clearing from somewhere else, somewhere in the forest.

Slowly, trying not to disturb the trail, Storm followed it toward the nearest tree and past it, into the deeper shadows. She sniffed carefully as she walked, hoping that despite everything she might catch a hint of something *other* than dog—a fox, perhaps, or even a giantfur.

But Whisper's fear-scent was the single overpowering smell . . . until her snuffling nose hit something wet, and cold, and the smell of blood filled her whole world.

Storm stopped dead, her vision swimming for a moment. When she could see clearly again, she looked back along the trail. There were smears and spatters all along it. But the smell hadn't hit her until right here, where there was a thick black stain and a small chunk of something red. It still had a few gray hairs attached. The hairs wavered in the air as Storm breathed on them.

She felt cold and strange, as if her paws weren't quite touching the ground.

She could see it now. Here in the dimness beneath the trees, it was almost as if the Sun-Dog was still asleep and she was back there in the night, watching Whisper's death unfold in front of her.

The light of the Moon-Dog shone weakly through the leaves overhead, glossing the fine hairs of Whisper's gray fur in a coat of silver as he moved in and out of the shadows.

He came that way, she thought, staring at a path that wound between the trees and the bushes. He was heading directly for the camp, innocent and unwary. *Why would he be wary? He was within our borders, almost within scent of home.* In barely a rabbit-chase he would have been out of the trees and in sight of the Patrol Dogs' den. He would have been safe.

Instead another dog had come out of the darkness. Storm wished she could see a sign, smell a scent somewhere that it could have been a fox, or anything else, but she was sure. It must have been a dog.

And that dog came . . . that way. Storm could see the route the attacker must have taken, flanking Whisper, staying between him and the safe, open spaces.

Storm raised her head and sniffed, but there were only the familiar scents of the Pack here—no trace of fox-scent. Dogs passed this way all the time, patrolling or dragging home their prey. No single dog-scent stood out from the others, except for Whisper's. His fear hung in the air, tangy and strong.

If it was a strange dog, Whisper hadn't scented it or seen it coming, not until it had torn from the shadows. Before he even knew what was happening, the dog's teeth had sunk deep in his throat. He'd had no chance to bark for help. He tried to struggle, but the killer bit him again, on his side, on his back, until he fell helpless at her feet. She'd dragged him into the clearing and raked her claws across his flank, rage lending her even greater strength.

She didn't leave him where he had fallen or hide him in the undergrowth—she'd wanted them to find him. She wanted the whole Pack to see him and be afraid.

When Whisper's last gurgling breath had left his body, she had turned and slunk back the way she'd come, blood on her paws, blood dripping from her muzzle. . . .

A drop of something warm fell onto Storm's paws, and she recoiled with a strangled yowl.

But it was just her own drool. She had been standing still, breathing slowly as she imagined the attack unfolding before her eyes, and a drop of saliva had fallen from her jaws.

Storm took a few stumbling pawsteps back, away from the pool of dark blood, and shook her head so hard that her ears beat against the sides of her face.

Wake up! she told herself. But she knew that this was no simple dream. Her vision of the crime was so clear . . . disturbingly, frighteningly clear. How could she see it so easily? It was almost as if she had been there.

As if she had been the murderer.

"No! Don't think that!" Storm whined aloud. Perhaps Lucky was right, and she was simply imagining things. *I was out hunting the Golden Deer. Lucky and Snap were with me. I didn't sleep, so I couldn't have been sleepwalking.*

Even if some dark urge had taken her over, and she had forgotten what it was to be a good dog, and everything that some of the other dogs suspected about Fierce Dogs was true . . . she could not have killed Whisper last night.

The body was cold, said a nasty voice in the back of Storm's mind. *He was found this morning—but no dog said he was killed last night.*

Dread pierced Storm's heart, and she turned tail and ran back to the clearing.

How can I trust my own memories? How can a dog who walks in her sleep know for certain where she has been, or what she has done?

CHAPTER TWO

The Sun-Dog was halfway across the sky, peering down keenly through the branches of the trees. Storm had watched as the dogs talked of revenge until there was nothing more to say, then slowly padded back into the camp in ones and twos. Alpha and Beta had not returned, and Storm had not moved from Whisper's side.

Some of the dogs had glanced uneasily in her direction as they passed her. But some dog had to stay with him, and most of Twitch's Pack was busy planning their revenge or patrolling. Despite Moon's insistence that they couldn't keep the double patrols up for long, five dogs passed by Storm on their way to check every inch of their territory for any sign of the foxes' den.

Storm seemed to be the only dog who felt capable of sitting still. Without orders from Alpha or Beta, the other dogs not on patrol were trying to keep themselves busy with small jobs around the camp, or by forming little knots of worried chatter at the edge of the clearing or by the pond. She couldn't always see them, but she could hear their whimpers and scent their unease.

One by one, they would come to sit by Storm and Whisper for a little while, their heads bowed and silent, as if each of them wanted to pay their respects but wasn't sure how. Then, without a word to Storm, they would get up and hurry away.

"How are you holding up, Storm?" a kind, quiet voice said now. Storm looked up to see Mickey sitting down beside her.

"I'm fine," Storm said, although she felt about a hundred rabbit-chases from fine.

Mickey nodded, and they passed a few moments in silence before he spoke again.

"We couldn't find the foxes' trail." He blinked sadly down at Whisper. "We saw where he must have been attacked, but there's no sign of the killer."

Storm scratched her ear uneasily. She ached to tell him that they never would find the foxes' trail, that she was sure no foxes had been in the Pack's territory last night.

Blade, Wiggle, and Grunt are all dead. Apart from Lucky, Mickey is the dog I've known the longest in my whole life. I don't want to keep secrets from him!

But her Beta had given an order, and Storm was a good Pack Dog. Anyway, trying to tell Lucky hadn't exactly gone very well.

"Whisper would have been so grateful to you for sitting with him like this," Mickey said. "I know you didn't like him the way he liked you, but you were a good friend to him anyway. We will make sure his death is avenged, I promise."

Storm nodded. "Thank you," she said, even though the words left a bitter taste in her mouth.

I wasn't a very good friend, she thought. *But now I will be. I'll make sure justice is done, somehow.*

Rake joined them, his thin shoulders hunched, and they fell silent. A few moments later, Twitch appeared between the trees and walked over to them.

"It's time," he said. "Whisper has lain here too long already. We must give his body to the Earth-Dog. Will you three find a place deeper in the woods and dig the hole?"

"Yes, Twitch," Storm yapped gratefully, dipping her head to the Third Dog. At least some dog was taking charge.

Mickey was the highest-ranking dog out of the three of them, but he and Storm let Rake lead the way as they left Whisper's body and headed out between the trees.

"I saw a good place when we were patrolling," the tall,

wire-haired dog explained, his tail wagging. "Whisper would . . .
he would have liked it there."

"Good," Mickey said quietly. Storm stayed silent.

After about half a rabbit-chase, Rake barked, "Here," and
stopped in a small clearing where the ground was spongy with
moss. The trunks of the trees were green and soft too, and smelled
fresh and slightly sweet.

Rake clawed at a patch of mossy earth between two tree roots,
and they began to dig. Storm pulled up a big clump of moss with
her teeth and then sank her paws into the damp ground. It came
away easily, almost as if the Earth-Dog herself was opening a
space between her paws for Whisper.

Storm and Mickey dug in silence, but after they had removed
a few pawfuls of dark earth, Rake let out a quiet whine.

"I never thought I would have to bury Whisper," he said.

Storm didn't know what to say in reply, so she just focused on
digging.

"After everything we went through together. It's such a waste,
for a good dog like Whisper to have survived as long as he did, and
then to die like this. Of course, you know something of what . . .
he was like. Terror."

Rake shuddered, as if saying his name was almost too much to bear.

"But you don't know what we went through to stay alive when we knew that our Alpha was a mad dog. When the Fear-Dog took him over, there was no way to tell which dog he would turn on, who he would scar or order to be starved. He used to make us chase imaginary prey that no dog but he could even see, until our paws bled and we couldn't run anymore. We should have risen up, I suppose, but—well, we were afraid. We were never safe from him. All we had was each other."

Storm paused in her digging to stare at Rake—scruffy, thin, slightly rebellious Rake. She hadn't realized, or perhaps she had just forgotten, that Twitch's Pack was bonded together in a way that no healthy Pack should have to be.

Of course they always seem to be fighting to protect Twitch's position— Twitch was one of us once, but he survived Terror too. He's one of them now, in a way Alpha can never be. No wonder they still act more like a separate Pack than a part of ours.

There was a rustling in the undergrowth, and Storm looked up, sniffing the air nervously. But it was only a patrol emerging from behind a bush—Breeze, with Daisy padding at her heels.

The two Patrol Dogs paused by the hole for a moment, watching solemnly as Storm, Rake, and Mickey continued to dig. Finally Daisy whined, "I just can't believe it."

"I know," Breeze said. She trod the ground in front of her, her claws pulling up small clumps of moss. "It's *Whisper*."

"I didn't know him very well. He was a good dog, but I didn't really *know* him. I always thought I would have a long time to get to know him better." Daisy flicked back her ears and blinked up at Storm. "I'm so sorry, Storm. I know that the two of you were good friends."

Storm hung her head.

I always found him irritating, when he was only trying to be nice. Some friend I was.

"Yes, Whisper certainly had a soft spot for you, Storm," Breeze said. "Our savior, slayer of Terror . . . he was so grateful for the new life you gave us all. You must have been one of the last dogs to see him alive, when you settled down to sleep near each other. Was he happy?"

Storm stared at Breeze. Of course, she was right—Storm *had* been the last dog to see him alive. Apart from his killer, of course. . . .

A jolt of fear and doubt shot through her, as that terrible voice that seemed to come from deep inside her spoke up again. *Last to see him alive. Are you sure you weren't also the first to see him dead?* She had dreamed that night, dreamed of fighting, and woken far from camp.

No! Storm swiped at the nasty thought, and it retreated again.

"Yes," she said softly, "Whisper had enjoyed the hunt that day. We all did, even though we didn't find the Golden Deer. He was happy."

"I'm so glad," Breeze said. "He must have suffered, when he was killed—it's comforting to think that his last hours were happy ones."

Storm turned back to her digging, scraping big chunks of earth out of the ground until Mickey and Rake were struggling to keep up.

She didn't find Breeze's words comforting at all.

Storm took Whisper's front paw in her jaws, shuddering as the taste of blood bathed her tongue. She tried to be as gentle as she could, even though she knew she couldn't hurt him anymore. Beta held Whisper's scruff firmly between his teeth, and Bruno, Arrow, and Rake took hold of his other legs. They carried him awkwardly between them, but Storm was glad that they weren't simply leaving it to Beta to drag him across the earth.

The Pack, including Moon, who had been permitted to leave High Watch, was gathered around the hole between the mossy roots of the tree, waiting in silence as the dogs carried Whisper's body to the edge of the pit and carefully lowered it down. Whisper's paws folded neatly together as he sank down into the earth. With a gentle nudge, Lucky tucked the smaller dog's head to his chest so that they couldn't see the terrible wound in his throat. He looked just like a young pup, sleeping peacefully in his Mother-Dog's den.

Alpha sat at the end of Whisper's grave, still and silent, until the five dogs had stepped back to join the crowd around the tree. As Storm backed away, Mickey stepped close to her side and gave her a tiny lick on her torn ear. "Well done," he whispered.

"Packmates, we are here to say good-bye to one of our own." Alpha's body was still, her neck and back as long and straight as her bulging belly would allow, but her voice wavered as she spoke. "Dear Whisper, who was taken from us far too soon. He was a good dog."

There were faint murmurs of agreement from the Pack. Storm saw Woody's enormous tongue lolling from his jaws as he panted, perhaps thinking of some happy memory of his old Packmate. On the other side of the grave, Omega's white fur was quivering as if she were standing in a strong wind, and she let out a tiny, quiet howl.

"He was always willing to help. He always wanted the best for his Pack. His death leaves a deep wound in all of us." Alpha blinked slowly, then turned her large eyes to her Beta and gave him a small nod.

"My only comfort," Lucky said, "is that he is with Earth-Dog now, running in the Forests Beyond."

Storm's ears pricked up, and she saw several other dogs cock their heads to one side or look at Lucky in surprise. She'd never heard any dog talk about the "Forests Beyond" before.

"You all know that before the Storm of Dogs, I was visited by the Spirit Dogs in my dreams," Beta went on solemnly. "I haven't had any of those dreams since Blade was defeated, except one. Right after the battle, I dreamed that I saw all our lost friends, running together as a Pack, in a bright-green land. Alfie, Martha, Spring . . . Fiery, and little Nose and Wiggle. They were safe, and they were happy."

Several dogs let out strangled whines and howls, remembering their lost kin and Packmates—Moon, Thorn, and Beetle leaned their heads together at the mention of Fiery and Nose, and

Storm looked up at the canopy of the trees, thinking of her litter-brothers. Wiggle and Grunt—Fang, as he had been named by the Fierce Dogs—were they together in the Forests Beyond, playing like pups again, hunting alongside the Earth-Dog? It was a wonderful thought.

"So Whisper's gone there too?" Ruff spoke up.

"Yes, I think so." Lucky looked across to Twitch, who was standing on the other side of Alpha. Twitch stepped forward.

"I know that some of us have had a hard time adjusting to life in Alpha's Pack," he said. The dogs of Twitch's Pack stood slightly to attention, listening more keenly to their old Alpha than they had to Sweet. "But Whisper was liked and respected by all dogs—whichever Pack they started life in. I'm grateful that he had the chance to experience a happy life in a free, stable Pack, at least for a little while. After the horrors that we saw under Terror . . . I'm grateful that we all have that chance."

He stepped forward, and with his good front paw, he scraped a pawful of earth into the hole on top of Whisper's body.

"Good hunting, Whisper," he murmured.

Alpha and Beta added their pawfuls of earth next, each repeating Twitch's solemn good-bye: "Good hunting, Whisper."

The rest of the dogs stepped forward one by one, Alpha's Pack hanging back to let the dogs of Twitch's Pack say their good-byes first. The older hunters went next, and then it was Storm's turn.

Storm scraped her lump of earth down on top of Whisper's body and tried to say the words, but they caught in her throat. Forests Beyond or not, the fact was that Whisper was gone. Wiggle, Grunt, Fiery, Martha: the Earth-Dog had taken them all. Why was she so greedy? Why couldn't she leave their Pack alone?

"Good . . . good hunting," Storm finally muttered.

She stood back and watched as, one by one, the rest of the Pack filled in the ground over Whisper's body—the other hunters, then the scouts, then the Patrol Dogs. Finally it was little Omega's turn, and she shuffled forward and patted down the last of the earth on top of Whisper. She hung her head and took a breath, about to say the Pack's final good-bye, when a yelp from Alpha made Storm jump.

All heads in the clearing turned sharply to the swift-dog. Alpha winced, and her strong and noble stance sagged as she bent her nose low to the earth.

What's going on? Storm thought, too panicked to think clearly. *Is Alpha in pain? Is something hurting her?*

"Is something wrong? Is it the pups?" Lucky barked, treading the ground anxiously.

Alpha looked up, her large eyes wide. "Nothing's wrong, Lucky," she yapped. "But the pups . . . They're coming now!"

CHAPTER THREE

Storm paced from the hunters' den to the camp entrance and back, again and again—as if treading over the ground would make the time pass faster somehow.

An anguished whimper split the air around the camp. Storm's paws shuffled to a clumsy halt, and as one the Pack Dogs who were sitting by their dens or the prey pile raised their heads and looked over to Alpha's den. Apart from Thorn, Beetle, and Ruff— who had gone back out on patrol at Twitch's request—every dog in the Pack was in camp. The anticipation was so thick that Storm thought she could taste it in the air. It made her fur stand on end.

Birthing pups sounded *awful*. Storm gave a shudder and went back to walking back and forth, her pawsteps speeding up. Alpha was such a strong dog, but even she couldn't suffer through this without crying out.

Storm had no real idea of how it would happen, nor of how long it would take. Alpha had only been in the den for a short time—the Sun-Dog had moved only halfway down the sky—but it felt like forever to Storm. Some of the older dogs had tried to explain to the younger ones what was happening. Bruno said he'd been living with his litter-sister when she gave birth to her pups, and all this was completely normal. Storm knew he meant it to be reassuring, but she couldn't help feeling a swell of admiration for all Mother-Dogs, and a rock-hard certainty that she never wanted to become one.

At least Alpha had Moon with her—Moon had had pups of her own and knew what to do. The older dog's reassuring voice could sometimes be heard from the den, in between Alpha's yowls. But the sound was nothing next to the scent of Lucky's panic, which burst over Storm's nose whenever her wandering feet took her anywhere near the den.

"Storm, will you sit *down*?" a dog snapped. Storm spun around to see Dart glowering down her long nose at her. "You're going to wear out the grass pacing around like that, not to mention driving every dog crazy!"

Dart's only a scout dog. She can't tell me what to do, Storm thought, but she knew that the slender brown-and-white dog was right. Storm picked a shady spot by the hunters' den, trod a tight circle three or four times around, and flopped down, blowing out her breath in a frustrated huff.

Alpha gave another loud howl, and Storm tensed with the urge to leap up again and run to her leader's aid. But there was nothing that a big, clumsy, young Fierce Dog could do for Alpha right now. Storm squeezed her eyes shut, but that just seemed to make the sounds ring louder in her ears. She wanted to get up and walk again, or just leave the camp behind and run and run. She wished she'd thought of volunteering to patrol with Thorn and Beetle, even though she was a hunter.

She felt trapped between Whisper's grave and the pups' den, between the end of a life and the beginning of new ones. It was as if the Spirit Dogs were panting over her shoulder, watching the Pack through her eyes, and waiting for her to do something. But what? What did they expect her to do?

Suddenly her nose twitched as fear-scent overwhelmed her. She snapped her eyes open and saw Lucky walking toward her. He was panting as if he had been chasing deer, and his eyes were wild and bright. Alpha's howls still rang out from the den.

Storm was instantly on her paws. "What is it, Beta? Is Alpha okay?"

Other dogs began to rush toward Lucky.

"Beta, can we help?" Mickey asked.

Lucky halted in front of Storm, and she could see that his legs were trembling.

"Alpha is doing well." He paused, then looked a little sheepish. "Moon made me leave."

"But Alpha—and—the puppies are definitely—" Sunshine faltered.

"Everything is happening as Moon said it should." Lucky sighed. "We just have to wait." He turned abruptly, as if he had an itch he couldn't wait to scratch, and paced away toward the other side of camp.

The rest of the Pack dispersed, wagging their tails at the reassuring news, but Storm felt even worse than she had before. Lucky's fear-scent was still thick in her throat, and the noises from the den were impossible to ignore.

"Storm, are you all right?"

Storm looked around sharply and found Twitch by her side. The Third Dog's floppy ears were cocked lopsidedly with worry, and Storm nodded quickly.

"I'm fine, Twitch."

"I know it can be frightening," Twitch said. "It's always hard when the Pack's Alpha is hurting. But the pups will be here soon, and then Alpha will feel much better."

"Thank you," Storm said, wishing that she felt more comforted. He couldn't understand what was truly frightening her. Perhaps even if he did, he would still try to offer comfort—but she couldn't tell him that it wasn't only her fear for Alpha that was making her jump at every yelp or howl of pain.

"Why don't you take some dogs and go out on a hunt?" Twitch said. "Alpha doesn't need all of us to sit around like lazy pups waiting for her—she's certainly going to need fresh prey to eat when this is over."

Despite the weight of her fears, Storm's ears pricked and she sat up straighter.

"Really? You want me to lead a hunting party?"

"Absolutely," said Twitch. "I'm sure you'll bring back something wonderful to help Alpha recover her strength."

"I will!" Storm promised. She cast her eyes around the Pack, and then trotted over to Mickey, who was watching them with interest. He hadn't moved, but as she approached he got to his paws and shook out his long black-and-white fur. "Will you come hunting with me, Mickey? We need to find some prey for Alpha."

"I'd love to," Mickey panted happily. "It'll be good to stretch my legs."

"Is there a hunting party going out?" said another voice, and Storm turned to see Bella and Arrow padding toward them, shoulder to shoulder.

"Yes. Storm's leading it," said Mickey, with a hint of pride.

"We'll come with you," said Arrow.

Storm blinked happily at them—three good hunters, plus herself. "We just need a scout dog," she said, and looked around the camp, hoping she could ask Breeze or Daisy. But Dart was lying closer than the others, and when Storm's eyes fell on her, she stood up and stretched.

"I'll be your scout," she said.

Storm tried not to look disappointed.

The dogs set off slowly, casting glances back at the sound of Alpha's whimpering. But as soon as she had the open hillside beneath her paws and the Wind-Dogs brushing against her fur, Storm's heart lightened.

Giving birth is something Alpha has to do herself, she thought. *But we can help her!*

She wasn't tired anymore, either, except for a lurking feeling behind her eyes that was easy to shake off as she broke into a run.

"Let's go to the meadow where you can see the lake," she barked to Dart. The scout gave her a sharp nod and split away from the party, her spindly brown legs blurring as she put on a burst of speed. The scout dog vanished into a line of trees, but Storm led the other dogs on across the grass, keeping the End-less Lake on her right. Their pawsteps thudded heavily against the earth, sending up small sprays of sand that had blown up onto the cliffs from the shore.

They soon arrived at the meadow and paused in the shadow of a large shrub to catch their breath. Storm sniffed the ground. There were often rabbits on this part of the cliff, and sometimes the big, lazy birds that flew over the Endless Lake made their nests here. She couldn't scent any of the birds now, but there was a definite hint of rabbit, and something else . . . something tasty.

Bella poked her muzzle carefully around the edge of the shrub, and then gave a low, quiet bark of satisfaction. "You've picked well, Storm! Look."

Storm peered over Bella's shoulder and saw a tall creature with long, graceful legs. A deer!

This was no spirit deer, either—the Wind-Dogs wouldn't lead

them on an endless chase like they had done last night. This one was real, and its delicious scent was carried to the dogs on a gentle breeze.

I wonder if the real deer is here because the Golden Deer is nearby? Storm thought. *Or is it just because it's the first New Leaf since the longpaws went away?*

Whatever the reason, Storm was grateful to the Wind-Dogs and the Forest-Dog for bringing it here.

Whisper had been on that hunt for the Golden Deer, too. Perhaps if she could catch this one and bring it back to the Pack to feed Alpha and her new pups, it would be a way to finish Whisper's last hunt for him. *It's the least I can do,* she thought, with a pang of sadness.

Storm froze when she saw movement in the field. Had they spooked their prey? She peered around the shrub and saw that the deer was just pawing the ground with one hoof, as if digging for the tastiest plants. The creature was still upwind of them. It moved off from its grazing spot but didn't turn and run.

"Mickey, you take the left flank," Storm whispered. "Arrow, you go right. Try to trap it, drive it toward us, and Bella and I will attack from behind." She looked around for Dart. The scout dog was nowhere to be seen at first, and Storm thought that she must be off checking the surrounding area, until she spotted a flash of brown tail that swished underneath a bush on the other side of the meadow.

Good, she thought, *Dart's seen the deer too—she'll stay hidden unless she's needed.* At least, Storm hoped Dart would have the good sense to do that. . . .

Mickey and Arrow melted into the undergrowth, their heads and tails low, treading carefully so their pawsteps wouldn't disturb any dry twigs. Storm sank down to her belly and peered underneath the shrub, trying to guess which way the deer would turn next by the movement of its spindly legs. Bella crawled down beside her.

"We'll be able to get close," Bella said, her voice barely a whisper. "We'll just need to stick to the long grass."

Storm nodded her gratitude to the golden-furred dog. She trusted Bella's judgment—on hunting, at least. And when it came to other things . . . well, if Bella and Arrow really *wanted* to spend all their time together and keep it from the rest of the Pack, Storm didn't see why they shouldn't, although she couldn't really see the point, either.

She focused on the deer, opening her mouth slightly and breathing as softly as she could as she and Bella crawled out from underneath the shrub and into the long grass of the meadow. Sunlight gleamed off the deer's flanks.

Storm's nose twitched as she picked up the strong, earthy scent of rabbit, and something else too, faintly familiar on the back of her tongue. But she resisted the urge to follow her nose—the deer was in her sights, and it was the better prey. A burst of rabbits fleeing from their holes would definitely send it running off. . . .

Suddenly the deer's head snapped up, and a moment later it kicked its back legs clumsily in the air and turned to bolt straight toward Storm and Bella.

What startled it? It can't have scented us—we're downwind!

Storm surged forward, abandoning her stealthy position—it was useless now.

Arrow broke through the trees on Storm's left, his pointed ears pinned back in annoyance. On the other side of the meadow, Mickey sprang out from the shadow of a bush, his tail swishing in confusion.

Storm focused on chasing down the charging deer, channeling her irritation into longer and more powerful strides. She swerved into the creature's path. Perhaps she could still take it down. . . .

But as soon as it spotted Storm, the deer reared up with a startled snort and bolted, moving as if the Wind-Dogs themselves were on its tail. It leaped between two trees and was gone.

Just then Storm caught a scent, the same familiar one that she had smelled back in the long grass. Now she realized what that musty, strong smell was. *Coyotes!*

Storm trembled, her tail instinctively clamping down between her legs. That had been the strange but familiar scent she had picked up in the grass! She forgot all about the deer as a vivid memory hit her—cowering under a bush, Mickey and Wiggle beside her, Lucky grabbing Grunt and dragging him into the mud with them, just in time. . . .

The coyotes would have eaten us. They ate dogs—or at least, they ate defenseless pups.

Storm shook herself and took a few clumsy but determined steps forward. She was no defenseless pup now.

"Coyotes! Dirty coyotes!" Bella snarled, and raced past Storm, following the scent.

Mickey barked too, and fell in step with the golden dog. "They made us lose our prey!"

Storm ran after Bella and Mickey, but it was like running through the tugging waters of the Endless Lake. She knew she wasn't truly afraid of scrawny coyotes—but her mind was still swimming in the terror she'd felt as a pup.

But when they reached the trees, there were no coyotes to be seen, only the scent they had left behind.

Bella made to plunge on through the wood, but Storm barked, "Let's leave them. We'd be better off saving our energy for prey."

"Coyotes . . ." Mickey shook his head, panting hard. "I hate coyotes. What are they doing here?"

Yes, what are *they doing here? Could it be . . . could* they *have killed Whisper?* But as soon as she'd had that thought, her heart sank. She knew it couldn't be true—coyotes smelled even worse than foxes, and if they'd been anywhere near the camp, she and Lucky would have known it at once.

"Didn't you smell them coming when you were scouting this place out?" Arrow asked, twitching an ear at Dart.

Dart bristled. "What are you saying? That I would scent coyotes and not tell you?"

"There's no need to get so sensitive," Bella said. "He didn't say that. They smell pretty bad, so they can't have been here long, that's all."

Dart sniffed, obviously not too comforted by Bella's explanation.

"Either way, they've scared off all the prey around here," Storm said quickly. She put her nose to the ground and sniffed, trying to find the scents of the rabbits under the smell of angry dogs and coyotes. She could smell where the prey creatures had been, but if they were still in the meadow, they would be hiding deep in their holes, and not likely to come out any time soon.

She raised her head and sniffed the air. "We should move on. Perhaps there will be prey somewhere in the forest that hasn't scented the coyotes and run off."

"I'm not sure, Storm. Maybe we should report back first and check on Alpha," Mickey said. He gave a nervous swish of his fluffy tail, and Storm realized that Mickey's memories of the coyotes must be quite different from hers—she had been afraid, but he'd had three small lives to worry about as well as his own. She couldn't blame him for wanting to get back to Alpha.

"We can always hunt again later," Bella agreed. "I'd like to get back and see if Lucky needs us."

All four other dogs looked to Storm, and she felt a small swell of pride. *They're still treating me as the leader of this hunting party.* Even though most of them outranked her, and the hunt hadn't exactly gone according to plan.

She nodded. "Let's get back."

I'll go out again soon, though, she thought. It pained her to return to camp without any food for Alpha, and her paws felt like they were weighed down with stones as she led the party back over the meadow, through the bushes, and over the rolling grassy slope toward the camp.

As they drew closer, Storm thought she heard dogs yapping to one another, and her heart juddered in her chest. *Is something wrong? Did the coyotes get past us and attack? Has something happened to Alpha?*

Has another dog died, like Whisper?

But a moment later, when she could hear the barks more clearly, she realized there was no fear or anger in them. The dogs weren't barking for help, they were barking for joy.

The hunting party came through the tree line, and Storm could see her Packmates standing with their tongues lolling happily, rolling on their backs or beating their tails against the ground.

Two small blurs of white zipped across the grass toward them—Daisy and Omega, yipping excitedly and occasionally turning in tight circles, as if their little bodies were too small to hold all their feelings inside.

"The pups are here! They're here!"

CHAPTER FOUR

Mickey panted happily and gave a little hop on the spot. "Are they all right? How's Alpha?"

"How's Lucky?" Bella added.

Daisy and Omega bounced on their paws.

"They're fine!"

"There are four of them!"

"Alpha's very tired."

"Beta looks like he's hit his head on a rock."

"But in a good way!"

"We're off to the pond to fetch them some more water!" Omega shot off, her little legs going at a speed that Storm didn't think she'd ever seen before. Daisy trotted behind her.

Bella, Mickey, Arrow, and Dart all looked at one another with bright eyes and then hurried into the camp, the loss of the deer

SURVIVORS: THE GATHERING DARKNESS

and the worrying scent of the coyotes all but forgotten, nosing their way between the other dogs. Mickey barreled up to Snap and rolled to the ground at her feet, inviting an affectionate, playful pounce from his mate. Dart sat down beside Bruno, her tail wagging against the ground so fast it sent up clouds of dust.

Storm watched them go. She was so happy for Alpha and Lucky. Of course she was. New pups! Her tail lashed slowly from side to side.

But something was stopping her from bounding up to the others and celebrating with them.

It's too soon. She knew that the pups couldn't choose when they would arrive, nor could Alpha, but still, Storm just couldn't bound and leap like the others. It wasn't even a full day since Whisper had been alive and well, running through the forest, annoying Storm with his constant presence. Now she felt his absence like a deep, dark hole that sucked away the happiness she knew she should be feeling.

She turned away from the camp, determined not to ruin the moment for the other dogs. She walked until she reached the mossy clearing and sat down by the freshly dug earth where Whisper was buried.

"Alpha's had her pups, Whisper," she said, though she wasn't sure why. Whisper wasn't here. He was in the Forests Beyond, with the Earth-Dog, and with Martha and Wiggle. Still, she felt like if she sat where his body was, perhaps his spirit would hear her. She knew it was a silly, puppyish thought. But she went on anyway. "There are four of them. We don't know their names yet. Everyone's so happy. But we haven't forgotten about you. I promise."

She felt a little better for saying it, even though she knew Whisper couldn't hear her. Storm sat alone and silent for a little while, and when the Sun-Dog's shadows had shifted a few pawsteps across the ground, she got up. Bowing her head to Whisper, she then turned away and headed back toward the camp. She should make sure someone had reported in to Twitch about the coyotes they'd scented, and now she felt as if she could face the other dogs' happiness without feeling like something was badly wrong with the world.

As she emerged from the trees, she was starting to look forward to meeting the pups. Lucky and Alpha were both strong, clever dogs—their pups would be good dogs too, Storm was sure. What would their pup names be? Would they be fast and wise like Alpha, or brave and cunning like Lucky, or could they be both?

As she approached the pond, she saw Arrow sitting there, his head bowed, staring into the still water. At first she thought he

SURVIVORS: THE GATHERING DARKNESS

must be about to take a drink, but he didn't move.

"Arrow? Is everything all right?" Storm asked, a worry pricking at the back of her neck.

"Oh, yes . . . it's just sad. That poor pup."

"What happened?" Storm gasped. "Is one of them hurt, or sick?"

"Not exactly. She's just very weak. Moon told me." He looked up at Storm and shook his head. "It's a shame. I'm sure Alpha and Beta will be all right. A litter of three is still good. I just wish . . . things like this didn't have to happen."

"What—what do you mean? Is she dying?" Storm pawed the ground and looked up toward the camp, fighting the urge to run to Lucky's side—if one of his pups was going to die, he probably wouldn't want dogs pestering him. "Is there anything we can do? What did Moon say? She knows about raising pups, doesn't she?"

"No, Storm, the pup's not sick. She's a runt."

Storm blinked at Arrow, confusion overtaking her worry. "Oh! But that doesn't mean she's going to die!" She gave Arrow what she hoped was a reassuring nudge on the shoulder. "If she's not sick, she might grow bigger in time. Alpha and Beta and Moon will take good care of her, you'll see."

One of Arrow's pointed ears cocked, and he frowned. "You

mean . . . you don't think they'll send her away?"

Storm just stared at him, completely perplexed. Arrow shrugged.

"That's what happened to runts in the Dog-Garden, before the Big Growl," he said quietly. "I . . . I had a litter-sister who was born a runt. She wasn't sick, just small. She was so tiny, she was almost small enough to curl up on my Mother-Dog's paw."

He gazed down into the still water again.

"The longpaws came. They were gentle to me and my other littermates . . . but they picked up my litter-sister and made their deep longpaw noises for a while, and then they took her away. We never saw her again."

"What was her name?"

"She didn't have one," Arrow muttered. "She was taken too soon. And . . . I think my Mother-Dog knew it would happen. Blade came to us afterward and explained that it was for the best. She said only the strongest Fierce Dogs were allowed to grow up in the Dog-Garden. It was for the good of the Pack, she said. To make sure all of *our* pups would grow up to be properly Fierce."

Storm shuddered. "A little pup can't survive alone, especially not one who's so tiny! Alpha and Beta wouldn't do that to their own pup." But then a wave of doubt hit her and she looked away.

They wouldn't do that . . . would they?

"What's the matter?"

Storm turned and saw Mickey and Snap, walking in step toward the pond.

"Are you all right, Storm?" Mickey said. "You both look like the Wind-Dogs ran right through you!"

Storm glanced at Arrow, but he stayed quiet, so she turned to the two older dogs. "It's just—one of Alpha's pups is a runt, isn't she?"

"Yes, but you don't need to worry about that," Mickey said. "She'll get stronger in time."

"Well," Storm went on, "Arrow says that in the Dog-Garden, the longpaws used to take pups away if they were runts. They were thrown out of the Pack. That . . . won't happen to this pup, right?"

The shock on Mickey's and Snap's faces told Storm all she needed to know, and she let out a long sigh of relief.

"Of course not!" Snap gasped.

"Oh, Storm," Mickey said gently. "I'm sure that only happened in the Dog-Garden. My longpaws would never have done that, and no dog would either. Alpha's pup will be taken care of."

Snap snorted. "Only a Fierce Dog would get rid of a newborn pup just because it wasn't as strong as its littermates."

Storm felt stung and glanced at Arrow, wondering if he felt the same when their Packmates talked about Fierce Dogs as if they were naturally more brutal than any other dog.

"Snap, that's not fair," Mickey said, and his mate twitched her short ears and dipped her head. "It wasn't the dogs who got rid of the pups, was it? It was the Dog-Garden longpaws. They don't sound like they were very good longpaws," he muttered. "Our longpaws loved us and took care of us when we were sick. They would never have done something like that."

"I know," Snap said. "I'm sorry, Storm, I didn't mean that. But you have to admit, it sounds just like something Blade would do."

Storm nodded. "It's all right," she said quietly, though she couldn't help but notice that Snap had only apologized to her and not to Arrow.

Still . . . I did wonder, just for a minute. I considered the possibility that Alpha and Beta might send one of their own pups away.

Is that because I am a Fierce Dog? Is there something in me that makes me ruthless enough to think that only the strong deserve to survive, and that the weak should be thrown out?

She shook herself. "Has anybody told Twitch or Beta what happened on the hunt?"

Mickey and Arrow gave each other startled looks and then shook their heads.

"No," Arrow said. "It was the pups—we were all so distracted. . . ."

"It's all right. I was leading the hunt," Storm said, relieved to have something practical to do. "I'll go right now." She trotted away, heading for the dens. The rest of the Pack was still mostly lying happily around the camp, all within sight of Alpha and Beta's den. Storm drew level with Thorn and Beetle, who were dozing together in a patch of sunlit grass close to its entrance. She paused for a second and sniffed the air. It was so strange—when Storm had left, there had been three dogs inside the den, each with its own distinctive scent, and now there were seven.

"How are they doing?" Storm asked Thorn.

Thorn blinked happily up at Storm and rolled over, exposing her belly to the sunshine. "Mother says they're doing very well, even the tiny one."

"Thorn was much smaller than me when we were born," Beetle said, without opening his eyes. "Now look at her."

"I was not. You were the small one!" Thorn kicked him, but without much force.

"I think they're all asleep now," Beetle added.

I shouldn't disturb them, Storm thought. *Alpha should know about the coyotes . . . but it can wait.*

She looked around until she spotted Twitch's floppy ears gleaming brown in the sunlight, and she headed over to him.

"Twitch, can I talk to you? It's about the hunt."

Twitch got to his three paws and stretched. "It's all right, Storm. You weren't away for long. I'm not surprised you didn't manage to catch anything. We'll send out another party in a while."

"That's just it—we very nearly did, and then . . ." Storm hesitated. The whole Pack should probably know about the coyotes—but she didn't want to start a panic, either, not when every dog seemed so happy and relaxed.

Twitch gave her a keen look, and then said calmly, "Shall we go for a walk to the cliff?"

"Yes," Storm said. "I think that might be a good idea."

She stayed quiet as they climbed the hillside, skirting the jagged rocks and patches of long, stiff grass that dotted the cliff top. When they'd finally reached a point where they could see out over the Endless Lake, with the broken reflection of the Sun-Dog glittering on the water, she told Twitch about the disturbing scent of coyotes in the meadow, and how their prey had been scared away.

SURVIVORS: THE GATHERING DARKNESS

"We haven't seen coyotes in this territory before, have we?" she asked. "They might have just been passing through. . . ."

Twitch shook his head. "I don't know, but coyotes are vicious, we'll have to watch out for them." He looked out over the Endless Lake, and his brows drew down in thought. "I don't suppose . . . I wonder . . . could they have had something to do with the attack on Whisper?"

"I wondered that too," Storm said.

Twitch cocked his head. "But you don't think so?"

"Well . . . They do have bigger teeth and claws than foxes—and they're crueler. But no dog has reported scenting them near the camp before. And their scent is so *strong*, we'd have known if they'd been near us. I don't think there's enough evidence to take it to the rest of the Pack."

Twitch nodded. "You may be right. The others are working hard on catching the foxes—it wouldn't be wise to split their attention, not without any real evidence that the coyotes are still nearby."

"So what should we do?" Storm asked.

"Alpha's right, we need to protect our boundaries. Increase patrols, and keep sending scout dogs out with the hunting parties. We have to be on our guard," he added darkly. "If those coyotes think we're taking their prey, they might attack our hunters. I'll talk to the scouts—they should know what they're sniffing for."

Storm nodded. Twitch stood up to go, and then gave her a lick on the ear.

"You did well, Storm. You reported back to me. We'll be able to protect ourselves better from now on."

Storm gave a soft, grateful bark of acknowledgment and sat for a while, looking out at the Endless Lake, while Twitch made his way back toward the camp.

Twitch was such a good leader. He never judged her, or made her feel stupid, even when her problems were a lot less obvious than coyotes on the borders. Whatever happened, he always made her feel as if the problem could be solved, somehow.

She could see why his Pack had turned to him when Terror had fallen.

I just wish more of my Packmates were like him. . . .

CHAPTER FIVE

It was so cold.

Storm's skin crawled with it, as if there were tiny frozen insects all over her. She tried to open her eyes, but she realized they were already open—and she was surrounded by pure pitch blackness. She shifted her paws, afraid they might fuse to the frozen black ground under her pads, and turned on the spot, searching the darkness for some sign of where she was or how she could get home.

Suddenly there was a light. It was far off, but blindingly bright compared to the darkness all around her. As she stared at it, she could begin to see that it was daylight on green grass. The forest, the camp, and the Sun-Dog were all over there, somewhere in the distance. All she had to do was get out of the darkness.

Storm began to walk forward and then broke into a run. Her breath came harder and faster as she ran, clouding in front of her in the freezing air. Her paws made no sound, though she could feel them slamming against the hard black ground.

The forest must be very far away—she had run a rabbit-chase or two already, and it seemed no closer. Storm put on a burst of speed, feeling like she was almost flying through the dark, but the bright-green grass seemed to drift away from her as fast as she sped toward it.

I must get home, *she thought desperately.* Back to the Pack, to my family and my friends. No dog can live in the dark, like this . . . their hearts would freeze and die. . . .

Storm ran faster, chasing the sunlight as if it were prey. She would catch it. She would outpace this darkness! She—

Something smacked into her forelegs as she bounded through the dark, making her stumble and fall. The obstacle was soft and slightly squishy under her paws. She scrambled upright, staring down into the darkness, trying to make out what she could have fallen over.

Then she jumped back, howling.

There were eyes in the darkness. Two unmoving gray eyes like shiny pebbles. The longer she looked, the more she could see—lifeless, cloudy eyes, set in a face covered with thin gray fur. A bloody throat and flank.

"No, Whisper . . ." Storm whined. Her jaws felt strange, as if she had a mouth full of water.

But it wasn't water.

She looked down and saw that blood was streaming from between her teeth. It coated her front and her paws. There was gray fur caught between her claws.

"Storm..."

The voice was no more than a hiss, but Storm recoiled from the body, her paws slipping. Slowly Whisper's lifeless eyes turned to follow her.

"Storm..." came the whisper again. "The darkness is in you! Storm..."

"Storm!"

Storm snapped awake, swaying on her paws. The forest around her was dark, but the Moon-Dog was shining down on her, and compared to the utter blackness of her dream, it seemed almost like daylight. The trunks of the trees swam in front of her eyes, and for a moment she thought, *I got away... I beat the darkness....*

Then she realized that the voice was real, too, and it wasn't a lifeless hiss, but an anxious whine.

"Storm, please wake up.... Can you hear me?"

It was Daisy. In the light of the Moon-Dog, her white fur almost glowed, and her wide eyes glinted uneasily.

"Daisy?" Storm said quietly. "I'm awake. Was I..."

"I think you were sleepwalking," Daisy yapped, and Storm's breathing faltered. "I was on patrol, and I saw you walking along with your eyes closed. You were whimpering. Were you having a bad dream?"

Storm hesitated. How could she say what she'd been dreaming

about? Daisy would think Storm had gone crazy . . . or perhaps she would see the danger of Storm moving around without being in control of her own teeth and claws. Maybe she would come to ask the same troubling questions about Whisper's death that Storm was trying so hard not to ask herself. . . .

But on the other paw, this was *Daisy*. She was such a kind, gentle dog. She would always think the best of Storm. And Storm didn't have to tell her everything.

"I was," Storm said. "It was terrible." It was hard to get the words out, but once they were spoken, Storm was surprised to realize she felt a little bit relieved. She watched Daisy carefully for any sign that she might be suspicious of Storm, but the little dog's expression didn't change from one of gentle concern.

"Oh, poor you!" she said, and Storm felt her heart swell with love for Daisy. "It's all right, Storm. The last few days have been hard for all of us. Whisper's death really upset you, didn't it?"

Unable to speak, Storm just nodded.

Daisy raised her eyes to the sky, and Storm looked up too. The stars were dim, and the Moon-Dog was low over the tree-tops. "It'll be dawn soon. You should get back to camp and try to get some real sleep."

"I will. Oh, and Daisy . . ."

"I won't mention this to anyone," Daisy said quickly. "I know some dogs wouldn't understand. We can keep this between us."

"Thank you," Storm said.

Daisy gave her another long, sympathetic look and then turned to continue her patrol. When she was gone, Storm made her way through the dark trees and found to her relief that she hadn't walked very far from the camp. The night wasn't too cold—not after the deep, black cold of her dream—and she didn't really want to risk getting back in with the other hunters and waking them up. So she sat outside the den, her tail curled around her back legs, and watched the camp. She could hear the snoring and snuffling of sleeping dogs coming from the dens. In the trees above her, small birds twittered loudly, knowing that they were safe from the snapping jaws of the dogs.

I can't go to sleep. The realization was like a splash of cold salt water from the Endless Lake across Storm's muzzle. *I don't know what I do when I sleepwalk. If I thought one of the Pack was an enemy... I don't know what I would do to them. If it had been a bigger dog than Daisy trying to wake me and I had felt threatened...*

She couldn't let herself fall asleep. It was the only way to be certain she wouldn't hurt any dog. She would have to find some way to stay awake. How hard could that be? Surely she could just keep moving and keep busy until she could snatch a few hours of sleep somewhere away from the Pack, where she was *sure* they would all be safe?

Storm sat outside the hunters' den and watched the light changing, from bright moonlight to the dim glow that came when the Moon-Dog had gone to bed and the Sun-Dog hadn't yet started his run across the sky. Finally the bright Sun-Dog poked his ears above the horizon, and long streaks of warm sunlight spread across the ground. Storm stood up to move into one of them.

"You're up early," said a voice from the den behind Storm. It was Bella. She sat down in another patch of sunlight and scratched behind her ear.

"I wasn't tired," Storm said.

After Bella, more and more of the Pack started to emerge from their dens and begin the day's routine, vanishing into the bushes to make dirt or running to the pond for a drink. Storm watched them, happy to be surrounded by activity and life. In the days since the pups' birth, the Pack had fallen back into their routines, despite Alpha's and Beta's absence in their Pup Den. Daisy and the other Patrol Dogs came back to camp one by one, their steps slow and dragging after a long night's watch, but pleased to report to Twitch that there had been nothing unusual during the night. Daisy glanced very briefly at Storm as she said this, but no other dog seemed to notice.

Then, suddenly, a bark rang out loudly through the camp.

"Packmates! To me!"

Storm was on her feet before she knew it, her hackles rising . . . when she realized that it hadn't been a bark of alarm. It was Lucky's voice, and he sounded joyful.

"Come on, sleepy-fur!" Thorn nudged Storm as she ran past. "It's time for the Den Break!"

Storm followed the movement of the Pack toward Alpha's den, slightly confused but starting to feel almost as excited as some of the other dogs seemed to be. They wagged their tails and jostled for position so they could see the entrance to the den.

"What's the Den Break?" Storm asked Moon, who had come down from High Watch to join them.

Moon panted happily. "Well, you know that Alpha and the pups have stayed inside the den since they were born?"

Storm nodded.

"The Den Break is the pups' first time outside. Their eyes have opened, and Alpha and Beta think that they're ready to meet the Pack!"

"Wow," Storm said. She tried to imagine having spent her first days inside a doghouse, and then being brought out to meet an entire Fierce Dog Pack.

She had passed her early days alone with her litter-brothers, exploring the Dog-Garden as much as they liked. The first older dogs she remembered had been Mickey and Lucky. They had been scary enough by themselves, and there were only two of them! She couldn't imagine how overwhelming it would be to face a whole new world and a new Pack all at once.

There was movement at the mouth of the den, and all members of the Pack turned their attention on their Beta as he walked out, his ears pricked up with pride.

"A Pack must grow to be strong," he said. "I am very proud and very happy to introduce you all to our new pups." He stood aside, and out of the dim interior of the den emerged Alpha, a sandy-colored ball of fluff held carefully in her jaws. "This is our male pup, Tumble!" Lucky said, and Alpha set the puppy down on the grass outside the den.

He was shaggy and golden-colored, and had floppy ears, just like his Father-Dog. But his muzzle was longer, like his Mother-Dog's, and when he blinked up at the gathered Pack, there was wonder in his large dark eyes.

A ripple of happiness and gentle excitement ran through the Pack Dogs. Alpha and Beta stood beaming at Tumble as he rolled over, then over again, and started to try to wriggle across the grass toward Moon.

"He's too young to walk," Alpha said, pride resonating in her voice. "But he doesn't seem to know that!"

Beta went into the den and came back out carrying another pup—this one was short-haired and tan, with the same long muzzle and dark eyes as her litter-brother.

"This is Nibble, one of our female pups," said Alpha. Beta set Nibble down beside Tumble, and she sat completely still, cowering slightly away from the crowd of dogs. Her jaws opened and she gave a high-pitched little squeak. The sound did something strange to Storm's insides—it was as if the ice that was lingering in her mind after her dream had been melted away and replaced by a warm, soft bundle of fuzz.

Alpha had returned to the den and was coming out with the third pup, who was even longer-furred than Tumble but a much darker brown color.

"This is Fluff, another female pup," Beta said, as Alpha put her down next to Nibble. Fluff sniffed the air curiously, then sniffed her litter-sister, then tried to sniff Tumble, but he rolled out of the way before she could reach him.

"And this is Tiny," said Alpha, as Beta emerged with the last pup. "She's another female. She was very weak for a day or two, but she's doing well now."

Beta put Tiny down next to her litter-sisters. The little puppy was about a pup-head smaller than her littermates, and slightly thinner, with short golden fur and pale, watery eyes.

As one, Tumble and Nibble and Fluff all shuffled toward Tiny. Fluff sniffed her, Nibble sat protectively in front of her, and Tumble nudged at her with the top of his head. She turned to look at him, and a little pink tongue no larger than a small beetle flicked out and scraped across the fur between his eyes.

The sight of the pups all gathered together made Storm's heart skip with joy—but there was a bitter twist underneath the sweetness.

I miss my litter-brothers. I miss Wiggle, and Grunt—when he was Grunt, and not Fang. He was a pain in my tail, most of the time . . . but he was my brother.

Perhaps I wasn't as kind to Wiggle as I should have been. I should have protected him, like these pups want to protect Tiny. . . .

Did we look this small and helpless when Lucky and Mickey found us in the Dog-Garden?

Twitch stepped forward and lowered his head so that he was almost at eye level with the tiny pups. They drew slightly closer together.

"Welcome, pups!" Twitch said. "May your teeth grow strong, your legs grow swift, and your hearts grow brave."

He drew back, and as he did, a ray of the Sun-Dog's warm light fell over Alpha's den. The golden and brown fur of the pups caught the light, and they almost seemed to glow.

"Welcome, pups!" cried Mickey, and other dogs joined in, turning their faces to the sky and howling with joy. Storm howled too, sending up her thanks to the Spirit Dogs for bringing the pups to them, for keeping them safe and well. A burst of joyful energy ran through her. She didn't see any Spirit Dogs in the scudding clouds overhead, but she could almost imagine them as pups, tumbling over one another, playing happily, in a time before trouble had ever bothered any dog. . . .

The Welcome Howl was short, and soon Bella and Bruno were dragging over the extra prey they'd saved for this moment. Alpha ate first and well—Storm imagined that having pups made you very hungry—and then Beta. Alpha lay down in the patch of sunlight, and Beta helped to nose the pups toward her. They obviously smelled milk, because a moment later they were all snuggled up to her and suckling happily.

The rest of the Pack tucked into the feast too, and Storm was thrilled to see there was enough prey for every dog to have their fill. Even little Sunshine found herself with nearly a whole rabbit, and she attacked it with excited determination.

"It looks like the extra patrols and the scout dogs are doing their job," Storm heard Moon say to Snap, as Moon chewed on a thick and meaty bit of weasel. "I haven't had any reports of foxes or coyote scent in days."

"What do you mean?" Lucky yapped, slightly too loudly, cutting through their quiet conversation. He turned to Twitch. "We should have had some scent of the foxes by now—I thought we had agreed to send scouts to find those mangy not-dogs! And what's this about coyotes, too?"

Storm's glance flickered to Twitch. Hadn't he told Alpha and Beta about the coyotes they'd scented? He must have thought they had enough to worry about . . . but was that wise?

"Beta, we have been stretched thin protecting the camp. There have been no more attacks, and no scent of the foxes at all—I believed it was better not to risk sending dogs away from the Pack to search for them. As for the coyotes . . . yes, a hunting party scented a group of them days ago, but there has been no sign of them since."

Lucky glared at Twitch as he gave his report. Twitch's expression was cowed in the face of his Beta's annoyance, but there was something defiant in his eyes too.

And he's right not to be sorry. His way of doing things has been working—we've had no more attacks, not even on hunting parties.

But then, I know the foxes didn't kill Whisper . . . and Lucky still believes they did.

An awkward silence fell over the Pack. Those dogs who were still eating stopped chewing, and several of them hung their heads or flattened their ears.

"Well?" Beta demanded. "Is it true? Have you just been patrolling, instead of doing as I said and searching for the foxes' camp?"

Snap got to her paws. "Yes, it's true. But, Beta, after everything that's happened and with the pups here at last . . . it's been nice to have a bit of peace."

"*Peace?*" Lucky gave an incredulous howl. "Is that what you want? Peace, with creatures who attack us without reason and murder our friends? Do you want to roll over and show your bellies to the whole forest? We must defend our territory! We have to protect the Pack! Our best defense is to attack the foxes before they return." He glanced back at his pups, and Storm felt a stab of annoyance.

He's panicking. He's a new Father-Dog, with four tiny lives that depend on him, and he can't handle it. But he still won't believe that the foxes aren't the real threat.

"As soon as we've finished eating, I want a scout party to go out and search for the foxes' lair. We must have vengeance for Whisper!"

A howl of general agreement went up from the other dogs, and Storm felt a pang of bitterness. She was glad that they remembered Whisper, that they were still angry about his death. She just wished that Lucky and the others weren't haring off in completely the wrong direction.

CHAPTER SIX

Storm kept low to the ground, ferns tickling her nose as she breathed. On her left, Dart crept very slowly forward, and on her right, Snap and Thorn lay with their heads pressed together so they could both see out through the same gap in the leaves.

They had been traveling for at least half a day—maybe more, but a blanket of clouds meant that Storm couldn't see the Sun-Dog to judge how far across the sky he was now—and they were well outside their own territory, peering into a scrubby clearing in an unfamiliar forest. A huge fallen tree trunk spanned the open space. It reminded Storm of the fallen tree near the dogs' camp, which had uprooted itself during the last Growl of the Earth-Dog. At one end, the spindly top branches waved in the wind. At the other, a whole colony of beetles scuttled in and out of the upturned roots.

Fox-scents were everywhere, seeping up from the ground underneath them, floating on the wind, even on the ferns themselves—the foxes had obviously crawled through this very gap in the undergrowth, and recently.

"We've found them," Snap whispered. "I'm sure of it. I've never smelled fox-scent this strong!"

Storm nodded. By the smell, this had to be the center of the foxes' territory. Their camp *had to* be around here somewhere.

The odd thing was that they had gotten this far without actually seeing a fox. Storm knew they were supposed to be cunning creatures, able to move more swiftly and quietly than most dogs, but it seemed strange that the patrol could have come this far without seeing a single one.

It also seemed strange to be out with two Patrol Dogs and one other hunter, but Storm could see the logic in it. Lucky had arranged the exploratory groups like this, with two dogs who could run fast and track the fox-scents, and two dogs who would be able to defend them if they found the lair. It wasn't a patrol, and it wasn't a hunting party . . . at least, not yet.

The dogs watched and waited. Storm glanced at Snap, wondering if she would order them forward into the clearing, or if they ought to retreat and try to circle around . . . but Snap was the leader, and Storm was intensely aware that they needed a strong paw in charge right now. If they started acting like Lone Dogs instead of listening to Snap, this could turn into a real disaster. . . .

Wait! Storm held her breath and listened intently. Had she just heard pawsteps? She glanced at the others, but all of them were pressed on their bellies on the soft ferns and none of them could have taken a step even if they had wanted to.

A moment later, the sound came again, and now it was louder. Dart's ears pricked up stiffly, and Storm felt the ferns under her body shift slightly as Thorn pressed herself even lower to the ground.

Then there was a movement in the clearing, and a pair of large red-furred ears appeared over the top of the fallen tree, followed by the rest of a fox. It hopped up onto the trunk in a graceful movement, although once the whole fox was in view Storm could tell that it wasn't strong or well fed—she could see the outline of its ribs underneath its red fur.

The fox had something in its jaws—a small prey creature, perhaps a vole, but it had obviously given the fox a hard time before it was caught, because its fur was mangled.

The fox didn't seem nervous—it obviously hadn't scented the dogs lurking right at the edge of the camp. It curled its brush around its paws and put the vole down on the tree trunk, then—

Oh. The fox glanced furtively around the clearing, then leaned down and began tearing at the prey. It threw its head back and swallowed the chunks down without even chewing.

Storm frowned. The fox hadn't put the prey in a prey pile, or even waited for any other foxes to come and join it before eating. Did every fox have to find its own food? What about the old or the sick, or foxes who just weren't very good at hunting?

The four dogs lay still, hardly daring to breathe, as the fox nibbled and tore at the vole. It seemed determined to eat every bit of meat it could, and after it had done that, it lay down with the remains between its paws and chewed on the bones for what felt like a very long time.

As Storm watched, a sinking feeling settled in the base of her stomach.

This creature didn't kill Whisper.

She had been fairly certain of it before, but now she was even more sure. The fox's jaw was even smaller than she'd thought— the wide collar of fuzz at the sides of its head made its muzzle look much bigger than it truly was. Its teeth looked needle-sharp, and Storm wouldn't want to have them clamped onto her leg, but they certainly couldn't rip out the throat of a healthy dog.

Between that and the fact that there hadn't been a whiff of fox smell anywhere near where Whisper was killed, she was more certain than ever that the foxes had nothing to do with his death.

What am I going to do? We've found their territory—Lucky will want to attack! But I can't let him start a war for no reason. . . .

But then, this wouldn't be the beginning of the war, would it? It had started when a fox cub had been killed and left near their camp. Storm had almost forgotten, in the rush and worry of the days since, but the Pack still didn't have any idea what had really killed the cub, or how it had gotten there.

Could the same creature have killed that cub and Whisper?

It was possible. The problem was that Storm couldn't think of any reason *why*. Who could hate both the Pack and the foxes so much?

The fox finally gave up on the vole carcass and hopped down from the tree trunk, licking its black lips. For a second, Storm thought it was going to try to come through the dogs' hiding place—but then it turned, took a few steps behind a patch of grass, and vanished. Storm stared. The fox den must be dug into the ground underneath the fallen tree! The entrance was masked by the grass, which was why they hadn't seen the hole.

This was the fox camp. They really had found it.

"Let's—" Snap began, shifting as if to crawl backward out of the undergrowth, but then she broke off and her eyes widened, her ears pricked up and swiveling, searching for the source of another sound.

More pawsteps!

The dogs froze, and a moment later two more skinny foxes came out of the forest to their right.

They passed close enough that Storm held her breath. One was male and the other, slightly larger one was female. They weren't carrying any prey, and they were talking as they padded toward the hole underneath the tree.

"Stupid prey," the male was complaining. "Stupid fast long-mice . . ."

"Better tomorrow," the other one said, possibly trying to comfort its friend. "No sulking, Fox Dawn. No point."

The first fox—was Fox Dawn its name? Storm wondered—reared up with its paws on the trunk, sniffed at the chewed-up remains of the vole, and then stepped back down. "Fox Ash had prey."

"Fox Ash faster than Fox Dawn," said the female with a shrug, and Fox Dawn gave a playful-furious snarl and snapped at her ears. "Come on. Den time. Long-mice will be lazy later, full of seeds, sleepy. Catch one then."

They slipped into the concealed hole beneath the tree and were gone.

The dogs waited a little longer, listening intently to the sounds of the forest, in case any more foxes were returning from their hunt. But there weren't any more pawsteps, or fresh fox-scents, and eventually Snap flicked her ears and jerked her head, and the four dogs crawled carefully backward until they were outside the ferny undergrowth. They turned and trotted away, keeping their silence until they had emerged from the foxes' forest into a wide field dotted with yellow flowers.

As soon as they were out in the open, Thorn gave an excited bounce on her front paws.

"We found them! Those mangy, scruffy little creatures—how dare they attack us? We'll get our revenge now, won't we, Storm? Beta's going to be so pleased with us," she added smugly.

Storm just hung her head.

"You don't seem too happy," Dart said, a flicker of irritation crossing her face. "I thought you'd be excited—you were as upset about Whisper's death as any of his old Pack. Now we can make sure justice is done."

"I'm not so sure this is justice," Storm muttered, before she could stop herself. She knew she had promised Lucky . . . but how could she just let this happen to those foxes, who were obviously struggling to catch enough prey to feed themselves, and who hadn't done anything to the Pack?

"Storm, what do you mean by that?" Snap asked sharply. The small dog stepped in front of Storm, blocking her from moving. "Answer me. What do you mean?"

"I don't think the foxes killed Whisper." It was a relief to say it out loud. "There was no scent of fox on the body or anywhere in the woods—no scent of coyote, either. And you saw that fox eating. Their jaws aren't nearly large or strong enough to do that to a dog."

"But, Storm," Dart said, "if you don't think it was the foxes or the coyotes, what could possibly have killed Whisper?"

Storm hesitated, hoping that the others' minds would catch up with their mouths before she had to voice her suspicion out loud. A second later, Thorn's eyes widened.

"A . . . a *dog*?" she whined. "But there aren't any other dogs in the forest, only the Pack . . . ." A small yelp escaped Thorn's throat as she followed the thought to the end. "No, Storm! You think it could have been . . . one of *us*?" She seemed so shocked that Storm almost felt guilty for suggesting it but nodded miserably.

"I think it might be the only explanation that makes sense. . . ."

"*Sense?* It doesn't make any sense!" Snap shook her head. "What dog could be vicious enough to attack a member of their own Pack?"

"Yes," Dart added, a sly tone creeping into her voice. "What dog would be *fierce* enough to do something so *savage?*"

Storm recoiled, stung by Dart's words.

"Dart, there's no need for that," Snap said, but her reprimand didn't sound particularly heartfelt.

If only they knew . . . I haven't ruled myself out, either.

There was no way she was going to tell them about her sleep-walking, her violent dreams. Still, there was another possibility that suddenly occurred to Storm, one that she hadn't even considered before.

What if it is something to do with Fierce Dog nature . . . but I'm not the right Fierce Dog?

She had no proof that Arrow wasn't the dog who had come out of the darkness to kill poor Whisper. Perhaps Whisper had done something to annoy him and he had snapped . . . Storm knew, all too well, what damage a Fierce Dog could do when the rage overtook her. She felt as if she'd been fighting to hold that rage back all her life, but Arrow had been in the Fierce Dog Pack. Storm shuddered at the memory of the Trial of Rage—the terrible ordeal Blade had tried to put her through, attacking and goading her into losing control and flying into a mindless frenzy.

With the help of Lucky and her Packmates, Storm had resisted the Trial. She'd failed, at least as far as Blade was concerned, though it had felt like a great victory to Storm. But Arrow had been a full member of the Fierce Dog Pack, and that meant he must have taken on the Trial of Rage and passed. Who knew what a dog like that would be capable of?

Then again . . . Blade's Pack had discipline. They didn't turn on one another unless she ordered it. Storm simply couldn't imagine Arrow attacking and killing one of his own Packmates.

The line of thought gave her no joy, but she couldn't stop dwelling on it as the dogs made their way back to camp. By the time they got home, Storm felt exhausted. The long day's march and the added stress of discovering the fox den had drained her small reserves of rest.

She could grab a few short moments of sleep before the Pack assembled to eat. She was getting good at it now. She hardly ever dozed off in the den anymore, and she hadn't gone sleepwalking at all since the night Daisy caught her. Storm felt proud of herself, as if she'd tamed some wild beast inside her. She didn't need to sleep like other dogs! Sure, she had less energy during the day—she reacted more slowly to things, and sometimes her vision blurred at the edges. But it was better than the alternative. . . .

She settled down, making sure not to pick a spot that was too comfortable, and allowed her eyes to close.

However, before she could drop down into the blissfully dreamless sleep she was craving, she heard muttering dog voices nearby. Storm peeled open one eyelid and tried to focus on the source of the sounds.

It was Dart and Snap, sitting close together right in the middle of camp. They were too far away, and they were talking too quietly, for Storm to hear their words. But she could see their faces, and their furtive glances toward the hunter den, where Arrow was sitting, cleaning between his claws with his teeth.

They had the same thought I did. But I talked myself out of it . . . didn't I?

Arrow finished his cleaning and stood up, shook himself, and trotted away toward the tree line. A few moments later, looking for all the world as if she was simply getting up to stretch and go for a short walk, Dart got to her paws and sauntered after him.

A flash of annoyance hit Storm. Arrow might be a suspect, but he wasn't the only one. They were only treating him differently because he was a Fierce Dog! What were they going to do, watch him all day and all night until he did something incriminating?

Storm shut her eyes and put her paws over her muzzle. She'd only wanted to tell someone that the foxes weren't responsible. She hadn't meant to accuse Arrow!

CHAPTER SEVEN

"Storm, wake up. It's time to eat."

Storm stirred and stared up at Thorn.

"Beta and Alpha have been in their den with the pups all day, so Snap is going to tell them about the fox camp when we eat," Thorn said. She looked a lot less excited about it than she had before Storm had voiced her concerns, and Storm almost felt guilty—not for telling the truth, but for taking away Thorn's nice simple explanation of what had happened.

Storm got up, stretched, and yawned. The Sun-Dog's light was deep gold and slanted between the trees into the camp, casting dark shadows and bright patches of sunshine. Storm didn't feel refreshed. She could have shifted into one of the warm spots and slept for another two days.

The prey was brought out—the hunting parties had done well,

but not quite as well as the day of the Den Break a few days before. Storm watched Snap carefully, wondering when she would report to Lucky. Snap had obviously decided that it could wait until all the dogs had eaten, because she didn't say anything until Omega had grabbed the last remains of a rabbit carcass and dragged it over to her spot to chew on the tasty bones. Storm felt her resolve harden. If Snap didn't say something about the foxes' innocence, then she would, promise to Beta or not. Their Omega dog was stronger and better fed than the hunters and warriors of that fox pack!

"Alpha, Beta, we have some news," Snap said. "Our patrol found the foxes' den."

Lucky's ears pricked up. "Good work, Snap!" he barked to get the attention of the others in camp. "Dogs, listen to me! Our enemies have been found. We will prepare ourselves to attack, and then—"

"Beta, wait," said Snap. Storm's heart swelled with relief and gratitude—Snap wasn't just going to let Lucky run out and attack the foxes after all. "We have concerns. The foxes looked small, underfed. We're not convinced that they could have killed Whisper."

A murmur of confusion rippled through the assembled dogs.

Snap planted her paws and looked at her Beta without blinking, but Lucky's gaze snapped straight to Storm. Storm swallowed, gathered up her courage, and stepped forward.

"It's true. Beta, I don't believe that they did. After what we saw today, I'm even more convinced. The bite marks on Whisper's neck were far too big to have been made by any fox, let alone these ones. And there was no fox-scent anywhere near the body! Think back, all of you," Storm insisted, glancing around at the rest of the Pack. "Do any of you remember smelling a fox there?"

"It's true about the scent, at least. . . . Beta, could they be right?" Bruno asked, shuffling his paws.

Lucky said nothing for a moment. He glared at Storm furiously.

I know I promised, Storm thought. *But you can't expect me to stand by while you attack the foxes for no reason. I just won't!*

"You . . . might have a point," Lucky admitted, though it seemed to be hard for him to say. "In fact, now that I think of it, perhaps we have it all wrong. If it wasn't the foxes, it could have been those coyotes you scented. We all know that coyotes will attack and eat dogs if they can."

"There was no coyote scent by Whisper either," said Mickey thoughtfully. Storm gave him a grateful look, glad that another dog—an older dog who Lucky respected—had brought it up.

"And Whisper wasn't eaten. It was like he was left there for us to find," Moon pointed out. "I still think it's more likely to be the foxes, getting revenge for their dead pup."

"But they're so weak!" Dart pointed out.

"I don't think it was either the foxes or the coyotes," Storm said.

The Pack turned to look at her. Storm paused, trying to think of a way to explain, but Lucky barked at her first.

"Storm, what is wrong with you?" he snapped. "Why are you so determined to say that Whisper was killed by a dog?"

The other dogs, shocked, began to whine and yap to one another anxiously.

"A dog?"

"What dog?"

"How could it have been a dog?"

Lucky took a few steps toward Storm, drawing himself up to his full height—which was now slightly shorter than Storm. Nevertheless, she found herself cringing down slightly and backing away as if she were still a pup.

"Do you want to accuse one of us right now?" Lucky barked fiercely. "Do you realize that by saying a dog has done this you are saying that one of your own Pack is a murderer? I've told you before, Whisper was killed by a fox!"

Storm forced herself to straighten and look her Beta straight in the eye.

"I am accusing no dog," she said firmly. "I have no evidence that any dog in our Pack killed Whisper. All I have is the evidence to say that it was *some dog*. Maybe it was a Lone Dog we haven't scented yet! Or maybe it *was* one of us—maybe it was a terrible accident, maybe that dog is sorry and wants to confess, but they're too scared. . . ."

Lucky advanced again, looking so furious that Storm almost thought he was going to swipe at her. Storm's eyes flicked to Alpha. The swift-dog was watching them closely, the pups held back behind one paw, her dark, clever eyes fixed on Storm. But she didn't call Lucky back. She didn't say anything at all.

The whole Pack was watching them, jaws open in shock or ears pinned back. Thorn was scraping anxious furrows in the earth with her claws.

"Beta, isn't it better to follow the evidence and find out if some dog has done this," Storm said, "rather than starting a war with foxes or coyotes?"

"We are not *starting* a war with the foxes," Lucky growled.

BOOK 2: DEAD OF NIGHT

"They have attacked us before. They believe that we killed one of theirs—that sounds like the perfect motive to kill one of ours . . . and no dog here had any reason to kill Whisper." He turned away from Storm and spoke to the other dogs. "The most important thing is that we are united as a Pack! We must stand as one, against our common enemy, and not let wild theories like this tear us apart. This is not a *Fierce Dog* pack. We don't fight among ourselves!"

Storm stared at Lucky. There was anger in his eyes, more than she'd ever seen there before—a fury and panic that he had never shown when they were facing Blade or fighting against the half-wolf Alpha. But now that there was a murderer in the forest, maybe even some dog right in front of him . . . he was terrified.

What he'd said didn't even make sense—only Blade had attacked her own dogs, and that was because she was driven insane by terrible visions of the Earth-Dog swallowing the whole world if she didn't. If anything, the rest of the Fierce Dogs had been *too* obedient and loyal to their Pack.

But the other dogs seemed to feel reassured by what Lucky had said. They were nodding, relaxing and barking to one another about foxes and coyotes, as if they were relieved not to have to think anymore. They didn't want to think that one of them could be a murderer, or that their Beta could be clinging to a lie.

She glanced across the circle of dogs and caught Arrow's eye. He gazed back almost impassively. If he was upset at the way Lucky was talking about their Mother Pack, he didn't show it.

But Storm couldn't hold herself back like Arrow could. She could feel the anger rising within her. Lucky had refused to listen to her before the pups were born, and now that they were out in the world, he was even worse.

I've depended on your advice, she thought. *All my life, Lucky, I've wanted your guidance, and your approval.*

Now I'm on my own, aren't I?

If she was going to be on her own, she might as well be alone. She turned, leaving the last bites of her rabbit uneaten, and walked away to the edge of the camp. Her fur prickled with the gazes of every other dog, but she didn't look back. She slumped to the ground in a deep shadow just outside the camp.

"We must defend ourselves," Lucky was still barking to the others. Storm wanted to put her paws over her ears and block him out, but she couldn't do it. "It's important that we stick together. You all know that bringing our Packs together has been a slow and messy business. Leashed Dogs and Wild Dogs, Fierce Dogs, Twitch's Pack, even a Lone Dog like me—we can all be part of something bigger, more important than ourselves. We just have to work together."

There were howls of agreement, and Storm gave a bitter huff. The trouble was, he was right. The Pack was more important than anything else.

That's why you have to protect it, she thought. *That's why you can't ignore the hard truths like this! How is it you can't see that?*

"We will train together, every day," Lucky said, his voice slightly quieter now. "We will make sure that we are a strong, united Pack when we face our enemies. And *every dog* will *know their place*," he barked.

Storm knew that remark was meant for her, but she couldn't even muster the energy to feel angry about it—she just felt desperately sad, as if a heavy stone were tied to her heart and dragging her down.

Her eyelids began to feel heavy too. She shook her head a few times, but no matter what she did, she couldn't seem to see properly—even with her eyes open, everything looked so dim. She tried to blink to clear her vision, but after a while she couldn't summon the energy to reopen her eyes. Storm's muzzle met the earth, and then there was nothing but darkness.

CHAPTER EIGHT

Storm jolted awake, her heart beating for a few moments like a terrified mouse running in circles before she looked around and found she was still in the hunters' den. There was a soft, speckled green glow in the den, the Sun-Dog warming the leaves and branches that sheltered it. She was alone.

Good. She had needed to sleep last night—she'd dropped off on the edge of camp and could have slept all night, and gone sleep-walking again, if Bella hadn't nudged her awake. The golden dog had wanted her to sleep in the den, but instead Storm had gone for a walk, treading around the camp perimeter until she felt she could sit without slumping back into sleep.

She'd been snatching moments of sleep all night, either huddled at the entrance to the den or sprawled on the ground outside, getting up to walk off the dizzy feeling of falling. At some point, the

Sun-Dog had risen and the others had emerged from the den, and Storm had thought it would be safe to go inside and shut her eyes.

She felt a pang of morning hunger, but the idea of sharing prey with the rest of the Pack made her stomach twist anxiously, until she couldn't tell the hunger from the sick feeling anymore. She would have to face the others soon, but she hated the idea that they would all stare at her, after her outburst yesterday.

It's not my fault. How can I be a good dog and stay obedient to my Beta when his decisions are so rock-headed?

Why won't Lucky listen to me?

He always used to—even when she had been a pup, she had felt like Lucky was on her side. Now, it seemed he only had time for one thing: his pups. It was as if he was desperate to protect them from harm, but the idea that the real threat might be from a dog that was close to him, a dog who was hiding true darkness, was too frightening for him to even consider.

Storm supposed she couldn't blame Lucky. She was asking him the hardest question she could imagine: Which of your Pack-mates do you think might be capable of murder?

She could understand him dreading the answer.

Lucky wants the foxes to be responsible, because foxes are outsiders—not dogs, who can be battled and defeated.

SURVIVORS: THE GATHERING DARKNESS

But wanting that wouldn't make it real.

Storm stood up and shook herself hard, from her head to the tip of her tail. There was a threat to the Pack, and if the other dogs weren't going to try to find out what it really was, then she would have to do it alone. She left the den and padded out of the camp, heading for the woods where Whisper had been found.

And if it's you? That persistent voice of doubt sneered into Storm's mind again, but she sniffed the fresh air and held her head high.

If it's me . . . I will face what I've done and take the consequences. What would those be? she wondered, a chill running down her back. Would she be scarred? Exiled? Would she be killed?

Blade would have executed any dog who posed such a threat to the Pack, but perhaps Storm's swift-dog Alpha would have mercy—if she thought the killer deserved any.

These were dark thoughts, darker even than Storm had become used to, and she pushed them away as she stepped into the small clearing where Whisper's body had been. Looking for evidence that she'd killed him would be as bad as Lucky scratching around for evidence that the foxes had done it—she had to try to keep an open mind. It was the only way to find the truth.

There must be something every dog had missed, something

that would point to the dog who had killed Whisper. Storm lowered her snout to the ground and made herself sniff all around the clearing, searching for anything that stuck out. The spot where Whisper had died still smelled faintly of blood, where it had soaked into the ground. Storm could make out the scents of the Pack as they'd crisscrossed this space, though she could tell they had been avoiding walking across the earth where Whisper's body had been.

Then, just for a moment, there was something. . . .

A volley of enthusiastic barks from the camp stole her attention away, and when she looked back, she couldn't think what it was she'd seen. It was just a patch of darkness that looked different, somehow.

She shook herself and tried again, sniffing intently for any scent that seemed out of place. Whisper's fear-scent lingered very faintly in one spot, and Storm hesitated. She could normally scent anger on other dogs—and the kind of fury that a dog would need to feel to kill a Packmate *should* have left a trail. But the only thing she picked up on was Whisper's terror. She shuddered. How could Whisper have been killed by a dog who felt *nothing*?

Perhaps sleeping dogs don't make scents like waking ones do.

Storm shut her eyes and focused only on her nose, trying to

shut out the sounds from the camp and the nasty voice in her own head. No more distractions.

I have to see what is really there.

When she opened her eyes again, the forest felt strange, as if Storm could see every leaf and every twig in sharp focus, but at the same time she could take in the whole of the scene in front of her. She felt her heartbeat slow down.

There. The dark patch she'd seen before and lost. It was a paw print, pressed deeply into the soft earth underneath the thin branches of a bush, where it had been sheltered from the rain and the passing dogs who had obliterated the rest of Whisper's last paw prints.

The print was small—about the right size for Whisper, too small to be Storm's own—and deep enough that Whisper must have been putting a lot of weight on it.

If he had been pressing down on the ground, scratching the earth in fear or tension, he would have raked the ground with his claws. There was no sign of that. Storm looked around for other prints nearby. If he'd been standing with one paw there, then the other prints should be . . .

But there weren't any other prints, until she looked farther, past the bush, almost hidden by the roots of a tree.

This wasn't the print of a dog standing in mud; it was the heavy tread of a dog who was *running*.

Storm followed from one print to the next, each spaced at the limit of how far a dog Whisper's size could stride. She could see him now . . . racing through the trees, some dog at his heels, his fear-scent blinding him to the smells of the forest. She could see his gray fur in front of her, beaded with sweat, and the way his ears flapped against his skull as he turned to look over his shoulder and his eyes went almost black with terror at the sight of her. . . .

Storm stumbled to a halt and let out a strangled whine. *Is this my imagination, or a memory?* She pressed her eyes shut again, but this time she focused on the hunger in her belly, the feel of the mud under her paws, the scent of the damp forest—anything but the vision of Whisper running for his life to get away from . . .

Storm's eyes flickered open and her ears swiveled as she realized just where in the forest she was. The camp was behind her. Whisper had been running *away* from the camp, away from the protection of his Packmates.

At her paws, there was another of the prints, and this one had something caught in the mud at one edge. Carefully Storm scraped at the earth until the little, hard, white thing fell out of the gap it had been lodged in.

It was a claw. No dog would have run fast enough to lose a claw if he hadn't been terrified, and no dog would run away from the Pack when he was afraid, unless . . . he didn't think it was safe. Unless he'd been attacked by something that came from within the camp. Her stomach turned as she looked at the little claw. It must have *hurt* tearing off. Something about it made Whisper's terror so much more real.

Storm sat down heavily on her haunches, breathing fast.

If I did do this . . . She stared down at the ripped claw, trying desperately to think clearly and not let panic sweep over her. *If I can avoid dreaming, am I safe, or is there no way to stop it? Should I leave the Pack now, to protect the others?* The idea was too painful to bear. What would she do? Where would she go? How could she leave Lucky—despite his anger with her—and the pups, and Sunshine, and . . .

"What are you doing out here?" a dog's voice asked, and Storm scrambled to her paws, slipping a little in the mud as she turned to see who was there. It was Bella, her head cocked to one side with interest and concern. Arrow was right behind her, as usual, his ears pricked.

"Nothing," Storm said. "I'm just . . . looking."

"At the ground?" Bella asked keenly.

Storm sagged. "I'm looking for clues. I need to know what

really happened to Whisper."

She waited for the two older dogs to tell her that she was being foolish, that she should listen to her Beta and not make wild accusations—but Bella and Arrow simply exchanged a glance and then nodded at the same time.

Storm blinked, distracted for a second by the fact that they'd seemed to talk to each other without making any sound. Could all mates do things like that? Perhaps it just came from spending so much time together. Storm didn't like that idea—her thoughts were her own, and no other dog was welcome to run around in them, no matter how much she liked their company.

"Do you need any help?" Bella asked, turning back to Storm.

For a moment, Storm was too surprised to reply. Bella and Arrow apparently took her silence for a yes, because without waiting for her, they lowered their muzzles to the earth and started to sniff around.

"I—I found this," Storm said, standing aside so Bella could see the paw print and the broken claw. "I think this means he really was running away from camp."

"And he wouldn't do that if he was being chased by foxes," Bella said, frowning down at the paw print. "I hate to say it, Storm, but it seems you may have a point. Let's keep looking. Maybe we can figure out what he was running from."

Storm thought about pointing out that there was nothing to find, but then she thought better of it. Perhaps Bella and Arrow would find something she had missed, or recognize a scent she couldn't. She sat down to one side of the trail of paw prints and watched as the golden dog and her Fierce mate sniffed and pawed at the undergrowth, then raised their heads to listen to the sounds of the forest, then smelled the air again.

Bella seemed to be searching aimlessly, but Arrow looked a lot more focused, tracking back and forth from the spot with the claw to the clearing where Whisper had died.

"He was attacked over there, where we found the blood," he muttered. "He was dragged into the clearing. He must have gotten up and tried to run—that was when he broke his claw. But he would already have been wounded. He couldn't have gotten far. If *I* was attacking Whisper, I could have caught him without even breaking into a run."

Storm flinched slightly, trying not to imagine the weakened, bleeding dog being followed by a merciless, unstoppable Fierce Dog. She wasn't sure which was worse, imagining that she had been the killer, or imagining that it might have been Arrow. . . .

"He would eventually have fallen—yes, here," Arrow went on,

passing Storm with his gaze completely focused on a scuffed patch
of dirt a few pawsteps away. "I dragged him back to the clearing to
finish him off. . . . I must have wanted him to be found. But why?"

Storm tried to shut out his words, wishing he'd chosen almost
any other way to phrase his question. Not only was it frightening
to imagine Arrow as the killer, it reminded her too much of how
she had visualized Whisper's death, how easy it had been to slip
into the role of the killer herself. Storm shuddered—was this their
Fierce Dog heritage? Then she felt warmth against her flank and
looked up into the large brown eyes of Bella.

"Are you doing all right, Storm?" Bella asked.

"I'm fine," Storm said quickly.

Bella tilted her head to one side. "No, I don't think you are,"
she said. Storm bristled but supposed she shouldn't be surprised
by Bella's blunt manner—Lucky's litter-sister never had any trouble speaking her mind. "You have every reason to be upset, after
yesterday. I know Lucky doesn't make it easy to disagree with him,
sometimes."

Despite herself, Storm let out a weak chuckle. Bella's descrip-
tion of her litter-brother was exactly right.

"Once he's gotten used to being a Father-Dog, he'll settle
down and see reason about all this," Bella went on. "It's just

happening too soon. He still thinks Alpha and the pups could be hurt by a stiff breeze, let alone . . ."

"A killer dog," said Arrow, in a muted whine. He padded back to where Storm was sitting and put his head close to Bella's. "I think she might be right, Bella."

"But the Pack's only dog enemies were Blade's Pack," Bella pointed out. "And the ones who survived the Storm of Dogs are long gone—you would have scented them if they were here, wouldn't you?"

"That's just it. The only scents I smell here are from our Pack. I think Storm's not just right about the foxes being innocent. We shouldn't be looking for our enemies—we should be looking at ourselves."

He caught Storm's eye, and her heart stuttered in her chest. *He knows. He knows! What do I do? Don't let my ears go flat—oh, Earth-Dog, I must look so guilty. . . .*

But Arrow's eyes weren't accusing—they were full of sadness. The moment passed, and Storm's panic passed with it. How could he know what she might have done, when she didn't know it herself?

"We can't take that to Lucky," Bella said firmly. Arrow's ears twitched in surprise, and Bella shook her head. "It's not that I

don't believe you. It's just that it's so . . . so *awful*. He won't be able
to handle it if we insist it's true. Not yet. Anyway," she added, a
thoughtful look coming over her face, "say we do convince every
dog that the killer is one of us. Lucky's right, the Pack could tear
itself apart—and the first dogs to feel the bite would be the two
of you."

The truth of this hurt Storm like a stinging insect. She felt
her heart sink, thinking of the suspicious whispering of Snap and
Dart. She had tried to tell them what was happening, and they
had taken no time at all to decide Arrow was guilty.

"There's something else too. If some dog in the Pack is a killer,
then they already know that you suspect," Arrow said, turning to
Storm. "You could be in danger. And the more we say, the more
we antagonize that dog."

Storm stared at him. That had not occurred to her, and the
thought was chilling.

"We need to approach this carefully. We must figure out if
any dogs were out of camp on the night when Whisper was killed,
and where they went," Bella said.

"But how can we find out any dog's movements without making them suspicious?" Storm asked. "I'm not sure it's a good idea
for Arrow to go around asking too many questions. He's . . . new,"

she added, not quite wanting to tell her fellow Fierce Dog that some dogs already suspected him. "I can probably ask around without making things worse—every dog already thinks I'm just a silly pup with a wild theory."

"Oh, Storm." Bella's ears drooped. "I don't like that idea one bit. But if you're determined . . . well, at least try to be careful."

Storm thought hard. Lucky and Snap had been out on the hunt for the Golden Deer when Whisper was killed, and Thorn and Breeze had been patrolling. Who else might have been awake?

Her tail wagged as a thought struck her. "Moon was on High Watch. She'd have a good view of the camp—maybe she saw some dog leaving their den, or something else that could help us. And I'm sure she won't go telling the other dogs I've been asking her questions."

"All right—why don't you go and talk to her?" Bella said, brightening. "And I'll ask a few questions around the camp."

"Promise me you'll try to be subtle," Arrow muttered. "I don't want any bad dogs targeting you next! If I didn't have you . . ." He trailed off, and Bella rubbed her head against his cheek affectionately.

"Don't worry about me, Arrow," she said. "I'm good at subtle."

Storm shifted awkwardly, embarrassed. "I should probably go

to Moon now. So we're not seen out here together." She got up and hurried away.

The fastest way to get to High Watch was to go straight through the camp, but Storm didn't want to meet any of the other dogs just now—let alone have to explain to Lucky or Alpha what she was doing. So she padded a wide circle around the dens until she reached the stony edge of the cliff, with its steep drop down to the sandy strip between the land and the Endless Lake.

She ran along the edge of the cliff, careful to keep a few paw-steps between her and the very edge, where the earth wasn't quite solid and an unwary dog could easily take a tumble down onto the rocks below.

High Watch itself was a bare, grassy space between the End-less Lake and the Pack camp, where the cliff rose even higher above the lake. A chill wind blew Storm's fur the wrong way up her spine as she climbed the hill and spotted the restless shape of Moon silhouetted against the bright-gray sky.

The white-and-black Farm Dog was turning around and around on the spot. At first Storm thought she might be chasing her tail, but then she wondered if she was turning a sleep circle. Surely Moon wouldn't go to sleep on watch?

She drew closer, and Moon saw her and stopped circling. "Good morning, Storm," she said. "Forgive me—I just need to warm up my paws." She went on circling, and Storm came close and sat down, shivering. The injustice of Moon's punishment hit her again, even more forcefully. *I didn't realize it was so cold up here.*

"I'm so sorry," she whined. "I know you didn't steal from the prey pile. I'm sure Alpha will let you come down soon."

"I hope so," Moon said, finally coming to a halt. "You know, Storm, I don't blame Alpha—I didn't steal that prey, it's true, but I understand how it looked. I'm just glad that I've been able to help with the pups. I think it shows the others that she trusts me."

Storm nodded and glanced back toward the camp. From here, she could see between the few trees that circled it, down to the dens and the prey pile, past the pond, and across the grass to the line of trees where Whisper's body had been found. Beyond that, the landscape rolled away from the cliffs, patches of grass and clumps of trees alternating until she could see the dark line of Twitch's forest on the horizon.

"You can see so far from up here," Storm murmured, aiming to be subtle, but unsure if she was succeeding. "If you think about it, you're the Pack's first line of defense—from longpaws, or foxes, or anything. You can see things coming long before we could scent them."

"That's true," said Moon, "but it's no substitute for proper patrols. Farm Dog eyes are keen," she added, with a hint of pride. "But they still fail me sometimes, especially in the dark. I didn't see a thing when the foxes killed poor Whisper. Of course, it happened beyond the tree line, so I wouldn't have seen anything from here, even in daylight."

"Oh," Storm said, trying not to look too disappointed.

"Still, I feel I should have known something was happening," Moon went on. "If I'd spotted a creature that shouldn't have been near the camp, I would have been able to bark the alarm, like you said. Perhaps . . . perhaps Whisper would still be with us. Or at least we could have caught the foxes in the act, and we wouldn't be struggling with not knowing if they had truly killed him," she added, padding close to Storm and resting her muzzle kindly against Storm's for a moment.

"That's all I want," Storm said. "Just to be certain that it was the foxes before we attack them. You understand, don't you?" Her stomach twisted up with anxiousness at the idea of lying to Moon, but she told herself it *was* true—it just wasn't quite the whole truth.

"You really didn't see anything?"

"Nothing but a couple of dogs leaving the dens," Moon said, and Storm caught her breath. "I saw two dogs wandering around down below—they must have been Pack members; they were far too close to be intruders. I couldn't scent them from so far away—they just looked like dog-shaped shadows. They walked off toward the woods."

"I see," Storm muttered, staring down at the camp with hope and frustration chasing each other around her mind. Moon had seen something that night, but she hadn't known which dogs she was looking at.

Was one of them Whisper? And the other . . . could it have been his killer?

CHAPTER NINE

The Sun-Dog was high overhead as Storm trotted into camp with a large rabbit dangling between her jaws. As uncomfortable as she felt around Lucky right now, Storm knew she couldn't avoid the rest of the Pack forever. Volunteering to go on the first hunt leaving camp that morning had seemed the best idea, and she had enjoyed the opportunity for a run with Woody, Bella, and Snap, Breeze circling them protectively as their scout dog.

Storm had channeled all her uncertainty into following Bella's orders, and they had caught several fat, juicy rabbits for the Pack. Now Storm was tired out and starving. It was hard to make herself place her rabbit in the prey pile with the others instead of gulping it down.

"That was a good hunt. Well done, everyone," Bella said,

nodding in satisfaction as all five rabbits were dropped in a delicious-smelling heap.

Storm turned away from the prey so that she wouldn't be tempted anymore. She was no fox, to sneak off with her prey and gobble it down all by herself. She could wait until it was time to eat. In fact, perhaps it would be a good idea for her to leave camp and lie down for a moment.

She was much more tired than she should be, after a single hunt. She felt as if she had been running for days without stopping. Her legs were slightly weak, and her breath was shallow. Her vision was a little bit fuzzy at the edges too, and she knew that meant it was time for her to rest her eyes for a few moments.

I'll just slip out and find somewhere safe to rest. I'll wake up in time for prey-sharing. No dog will miss me. . . .

But just as Storm reached the edge of the camp, she heard two sets of heavy pawsteps thudding against the ground. Looking across the wavering grass toward the forest, she saw two dogs running full pelt toward the camp, their long fur streaming behind them. It was Thorn and Beetle, and as they came closer, they started barking.

"Alpha! Beta! We need you, come quick!"

They raced past Storm and into the camp, yapping anxiously.

Lucky bounded out of his den, anger and fear mingling in his eyes.

"What's going on? Alpha's resting, and you'll wake the pups!"

"Beta," Thorn gasped, "it's the foxes! We saw them!"

"What, where?" Lucky growled.

"Near Twitch's old forest! We heard them and smelled them!"

"There were lots," Beetle added. "They were gathering together—we think they're going to attack!"

"What?" Storm couldn't help her whine of confusion. She opened her mouth to speak again but forced herself to stop before she could blurt out the flood of thoughts that were filling up her head.

That doesn't make any sense. They must have scented us near their territory. Why would they try to attack? They're weak, and they know we're more than a match for them in battle.

The rest of the dogs gathered around, muttering to one another and looking angry and frightened. Any doubt they'd had about the foxes' guilt seemed to be seeping away.

"Those mangy little . . ." Mickey's jaws clenched as he padded over. "First they kill Whisper, now they want to attack the rest of the Pack?"

"It's because of the pups," Breeze gasped. "They've scented them, and they know we're vulnerable right now."

Lucky's eyes went wide with fear. "We need to deal with this," he said. "And quickly."

"Drive them off!" Snap barked. "Let's go right now, and show them what it means to come into our territory!"

There was a howl of agreement from several of the other dogs. Storm looked around, from one dog to the next, waiting for one of them to notice what she had—that it didn't make any sense for the foxes to attack now.

Finally Bella stepped forward. "I don't understand. What could they gain from this?" she said, padding up to Lucky and catching his roving, angry gaze. "Pups or no, we've defeated them before, and we'll do it again."

Lucky frowned. "Yes, why would they pick a fight now?"

Storm's heart swelled with gratitude for Bella's ability to get through to her litter-brother when few dogs could.

He's actually considering it. . . .

"But we scented them! They were really close," Beetle whined.

"Well . . . if they are really out there . . ." Bella turned and fixed Storm with a look, and gave a tiny shake of her head. "If Thorn and Beetle really saw them, we should run them off, whether or not they're planning to attack."

Storm's heart sank, but she supposed Bella was right—whatever reason the foxes had for coming into their territory, it couldn't be good, even if they were innocent of Whisper's death.

Woody ground his large forepaws into the dirt. "We must fight them now. Those pathetic not-dogs may have some reason for moving now that we don't know about, but if they think we're vulnerable, then they're mistaken."

"Right!" Rake stepped up beside Woody. "They must not expect us to put up much of a fight. So why not let them come to us? We can lie in wait for them here and rip them to pieces when they try to attack. Revenge for Whisper, at last!"

"We all want justice for Whisper," yapped a small voice, and Storm looked down to see Daisy, her white fur bristling. "But that doesn't mean we should bring violence into the camp. Alpha is still recovering, and the pups are too small to be taken to safety."

"We can protect them," growled Ruff. The former Omega joined Woody and Rake, her small black form looking almost puppyish between the two taller dogs. "We won't let any more of our Packmates get hurt by those horrible beasts!"

"Ruff is right. The best way to protect ourselves is to finish this now," Breeze said. "Let them come to us, and we'll teach them a lesson they won't forget. We faced Blade's Fierce Dogs, didn't we? If we could fight them, we can certainly drive a Pack of starving foxes off *our own* territory."

"That's not a good idea." Mickey's voice was reasonable, but insistent. "If we're going to attack them, we should take it to their territory, not ours."

"Just like a dog from the half wolf's Pack," Ruff muttered, glaring at Mickey. "Thinking you know best."

Storm took half a pawstep back, her heart hammering. It seemed like, in the blink of an eye, the Pack had divided right down the middle—dogs from Twitch's old group huddling together on one side of Lucky, with those from Alpha's Pack gathered uncertainly on the other.

Woody leaned forward to glare at Lucky. "You were quick to turn to us for help when the Storm of Dogs was upon you, but now that one of *us* has been killed . . ."

"Now, that's not fair." Twitch stepped firmly between Woody and Lucky. "Alpha and Beta want justice for Whisper as much as any of us."

"We're one Pack now," Mickey barked. "Every dog feels the pain of losing Whisper."

Storm felt her hackles rise. What were they all doing? Arguing over who was saddest, when there were foxes acting suspiciously and a killer on the loose? That wasn't what Whisper would have wanted. He would have wanted them to catch the real killer, not argue about whether to attack the foxes or lure them into camp. . . .

She started forward, unsure what she would say but determined to give them all a piece of her mind.

"Storm, no," came a soft growl. Storm looked over her shoulder. It was Arrow. He jerked his head to the side and then padded away. Storm paused for a moment, still not sure that she wouldn't rather jump snapping into the middle of the raging argument and bark her fury at the dogs until they all calmed down, but then she turned and followed him.

Arrow led her over to the shadow of a tree and sat looking down the slope toward the pond and the tree line, where Thorn and Beetle had come running back to camp. Storm stayed on her paws, feeling slightly awkward. The others went on arguing, and Storm caught barks about "Pack loyalty!" and "Revenge!" but she tried not to listen.

"I know how you're feeling," Arrow said calmly. Storm huffed through her nose and resisted the urge to tell him that he had absolutely no idea how she was feeling. "Well, perhaps not exactly," he conceded, "but I know you feel like jumping in and telling them all to go chase a rabbit off the cliff. You can't do that. Remember, if you sound like you're standing up for the foxes, other dogs might start pointing their noses toward *you*."

Storm clawed the ground. "I know." A wave of frustration and tiredness washed over her and she sank down onto her belly.

A moment later, a loud howl broke through the cacophony of barks and whimpers.

"Enough!"

It was Lucky. Storm got up and turned to better hear what he would say, feeling resigned. Bella and Arrow were right—there was nothing she could do right now without making everything worse.

"That's enough," said Lucky. "I've made my decision. Bella, you and a few good fighters will stay here with Alpha and the pups. The rest of us will go and find these foxes. We'll drive them off our territory, and perhaps we'll even get to the bottom of what happened to Whisper. It's time those filthy fiends learned that attacking dogs will bring swift and certain vengeance."

A chorus of approving barks broke out around him, and Storm was glad to see that they came from Twitch's Pack as well as Alpha's.

"We should sink our teeth into every fox we find," Woody growled.

"I hope it won't come to that," said Daisy quietly. "It should be easy enough to scare them off."

Storm looked to Lucky, hoping he would echo Daisy's words—but their Beta just stared coolly into the distance for a moment.

"We'll do whatever we have to," he said finally. "To keep our Pack safe."

The other dogs seemed satisfied with this, but Storm didn't feel reassured. She was still looking at the cold, ruthless glint in Lucky's eyes, and feeling a chill of realization—that becoming a Father-Dog really had changed him.

"Daisy, Sunshine, Ruff, you stay with me," Bella was saying. "Moon, Beetle, Bruno, and Breeze—will you stay, too? And Arrow, I think," she added. "We might need the extra fighter."

Woody made a *humph* sound and frowned at Bella. "Are you sure that's a good idea?"

Storm glanced at Arrow, wondering if this conversation bothered him, but his face was placid.

"And why not?" Bella snapped.

"Well, it's just . . . the *pups*." Woody cast a worried glance back at Arrow, who still didn't react. "I'm not sure I would be so . . . trusting."

Bella's hackles went up. Storm thought she was only just restraining herself from giving Woody a sharp bite on the ear.

"Arrow will be of more use coming with us on the raid," Lucky said, before she could reply. "There's not much more frightening than a Fierce Dog."

He said it so casually, as if it was a compliment. Bella shot an angry look at her litter-brother, and then at Arrow, but the Fierce Dog still sat quietly, with only the tiniest shake of his head to tell Bella not to protest their Beta's decision.

Storm tried to follow Arrow's lead, but Lucky's attitude still grated on her—when it came to protecting the Pack, their supposed savagery was suddenly of value.

Sometimes they think we're more Fierce than Dog.

The raiding party moved at a swift walk through the trees, their ears pricked and their eyes scanning the undergrowth for any sign of red fur. Lucky led them, walking at such a pace that Storm kept thinking he was about to burst into a run. He occasionally lowered his muzzle to sniff at the ground, but his paws never faltered.

Arrow, Rake, Woody, Thorn, Mickey, and Snap trotted after him, and Dart circled them, using her superior scout dog speed to sneak quickly between the tree trunks, her eyes and ears open for any sign of the foxes.

Storm was bringing up the rear, but as they passed out from

the forest into a grassy space, she quickened her pace and slipped past the others, drawing level with Lucky.

They were nearly at the foxes' camp, and something wasn't right. They hadn't met the foxes Thorn had seen—the young dog had seemed perplexed when they'd traveled past Twitch's forest and farther, saying that she and her litter-brother had spotted them closer to the camp than this.

Have we walked right past them? Storm wondered. *Is this their plan, to lure us away from the camp so they can sneak around us and attack when it's vulnerable?* Then she reminded herself that Bella, Moon, Bruno, and the others were still there, ready to fight to protect Alpha and the pups . . . if any foxes showed up.

Storm glanced at Lucky, whose eyes were fixed on the other side of the meadow, where the forest grew thick again.

"Beta," she said, uncertain how to say what was in her heart without simply making Lucky angry, but determined to try. "Every dog is so . . . so tense. We must be calm, when we find the foxes' camp, right? Otherwise we could make mistakes. Deadly ones."

"Worried about me, pup?" Lucky asked, and to Storm's intense relief, there was a hint of humor in his bark. "Don't be—I know what we're risking here, but we have good dogs with us, and I think I can keep myself in check. You should trust my judgment,

Storm. I'm only trying to look out for you."

"I do . . ." Storm said, and took a breath. *But I worry that your terror of something happening to your pups has you seeing danger and threats where there might be none. . . .*

Before she could work out how she could—or whether she should—warn Lucky of her worries, the Beta came to a dead stop, sniffing the air, his fur rippling. A second later, Storm smelled it too.

Foxes. Lots of them.

They had arrived at the foxes' camp.

CHAPTER TEN

"The camp is surrounded by thick bushes with sharp thorns and nettles," Snap told Lucky, her voice low and soft. "We won't be able to charge them."

"And their den is at the bottom of a hole in the ground, underneath the big fallen tree," Thorn added, in the same quiet tone. "We don't know how far down it goes—there might even be another way out."

Lucky nodded. "Let's hang back." He led the dogs behind a thicket, and they huddled down on their bellies, staying low. "I have a plan," Lucky said, still keeping his voice down. "With any luck, we can get out of this without having to fight. We'll spread out around the camp, and on my signal, you'll all make yourselves as frightening as possible. We might be able to scare the foxes into moving on and leaving us alone."

Storm's fur trembled with relief at hearing their Beta propose a bloodless plan. A wave of tiredness washed over her as she let herself relax a little.

"But what about Whisper?" Rake whined. "I thought we were going to get *revenge!*"

"We should use our advantage," Woody said. "Tell them they must hand over the murderer to face our Pack's justice. If they can give us the bad fox, we'll let the rest go. If not . . ."

Storm squirmed against the damp earth. What would the Pack's "justice" be, for a fox?

What would justice be for me? If they suspected her, would the Pack Dogs hold her down while she was clawed or bitten? Would they simply leave a jagged scar across her flank, or would they go for the throat? And would it be Alpha herself dealing the blow, or . . . would it be Lucky?

"No," Lucky said, and Storm's relief jolted her away from the dark path her thoughts were walking. "I want justice as much as you do—but what I want more is for the Pack, *all* of us, to be safe in the long run. That means getting rid of the foxes for good, not starting another fight."

Storm's tail wagged involuntarily at Lucky's words. He was speaking sense! Of course, he still believed that if the foxes left,

Whisper's killer would be gone too . . . but that was a problem she would have to deal with another time.

Woody and Rake both growled deep in their throats. "If it was one of *your* Pack . . ." Rake began.

"Whisper *was* one of my Pack!" Lucky snarled back. He lowered his voice again. "And so are you. I am the ranking dog here, and we'll be following my plan. Any dog who doesn't like it can walk away now."

Rake and Woody both looked away. There was a tense silence, and then Lucky's tail thumped twice against the ground.

"Good," he said. "Storm, Arrow, you split up and take flanking positions on either side of the fallen tree. If they think they're surrounded by Fierce Dogs, it will make them feel weak and uneasy—and they'll be more likely to surrender."

A murmur of agreement passed through the other raiding dogs. It still irked Storm a little, to hear Lucky make such sweeping statements about Fierce Dogs, even if he meant it well. But at that moment she was feeling too relieved to do more than give a small sigh as she nodded to Lucky and got to her paws wearily.

"Get into position and wait until I give the signal, then come into the clearing," Lucky said. "And look as fearsome as you can.

The rest of you will stand with me and bare your teeth. Be frightening."

Arrow got to his paws, and they crept out from the dogs' hiding place. Without a word or a glance back at Storm, Arrow padded away from her and vanished into the thicket. Storm circled around it until she thought she'd gone about halfway, then pushed through the thick undergrowth toward the fallen tree.

She crept toward the foxes' den as quietly as she could, though in the stillness she felt like nearly every step was making enough noise to bring all the foxes running. Fierce Dogs were built for speed and strength, not stealth. But she went on, placing her paws as carefully as she could, getting down on her belly to wriggle underneath thornbushes and pressing close to the trunks of trees where the warning scent of foxes stung her nose. She was tense with excitement, but still so tired, her legs heavy with weariness.

The others approached the foxes' den from the front, crawling under the same bushes that the exploring patrol had a few days before. Storm couldn't see them, but she could scent them. Lucky had better make his move soon, or . . .

"Foxes! Come out and face us!" Lucky's bark echoed between the trees. Storm heard yowling and scuffling from the empty clearing, but no foxes appeared. "I said, come out, or we will dig into your den and find you!" Lucky cried.

The noise grew louder, and then a flood of red fur burst from the hole beneath the fallen tree. One, three, five . . . Storm counted ten foxes, all of them full-grown, their fur puffed up with fear and anger.

"Dogses!" one of the foxes yapped. "Nasty attack-dogses! Leaves fox-home, or we rips their throats!"

Lucky came forward, out from under the thorns, and stood in front of the foxes. Rake, Woody, Mickey, Thorn, and Snap all followed him. They made an impressive Pack as they bared their teeth, silently backing up their leader.

"Foxes," Lucky said again, with the barest hint of a growl in his voice. "You have plagued this territory for too long. We will not tolerate you anymore. This place is ours. Leave now, and never return."

Storm was certain the foxes would heed the Beta's threat. But instead of cowering back, the not-dogs howled incredulously, forming a line. Storm tensed, crouching to spring as soon as Lucky gave the word. *Don't leave it too long,* she thought. *I don't think these foxes are going to scare that easily. . . .*

"Ours!" one of the foxes barked back. Storm realized, with a small twist of anxiety, that it was Fox Dawn, the creature she had seen complaining that he hadn't caught any prey. "Ours before yours! Terrible dogs, mad, bad dogs! Kills our cubs, steals our foods!"

"No more!" shrieked Fox Ash, the thin female Storm had seen eating her catch on top of the fallen tree. "We stand!"

And without another word, the foxes leaped toward Lucky.

Storm burst from the thicket as Fox Dawn's jaws clamped down on Lucky's leg. Lucky gave a volley of angry, pained barks, grabbed the fox's scruff in his jaws, and tore him off. Storm snapped at Fox Ash, forcing her to cower back.

The other dogs had been so stunned by the foxes' attack they couldn't move, but now they came to their senses and leaped into the fray, snapping and snarling.

Arrow burst out of his hiding place and scrambled over the fallen tree in a flash of black and tan and teeth and muscle. The foxes yapped and backed away from him. Storm surged forward too, growling. Most of the foxes stepped and rolled to avoid her, but two of them glared at her with fire in their eyes and charged.

Storm yipped in pain as their teeth and claws latched onto her back. She bucked and kicked out with her hind legs, tossing her head, trying to throw them off. There were more small bursts of pain from where their claws caught in her skin as they went flying, but then the weight was gone and the two foxes were sprawling in the long grass.

A third fox charged at her, but she reared back and brought a forepaw down across its muzzle. The fox was knocked off its feet hard, and its head hit the ground and bounced. It lay still—not dead, Storm could see, its thin ribs still heaving as it panted, but its eyes were glazed. The fox was stunned.

Storm stepped back, catching her breath. She was flagging, her muscles aching and her vision slightly fuzzy. She should have slept more—but how could she have known?

Win the fight. Keep them down. Then you can rest....

She turned her back on the fox, looking to the others, trying to see through the flying dust and fur and the rolling, swiping dogs and not-dogs to see which Packmate needed her help.

But before she could step forward, something pierced deep into her hind leg.

"Argh!" Storm howled, twisting around. It was the fox—the one she'd thought she'd stunned—with its jaws clamped firmly on the back of Storm's leg, tearing deep through the skin and into the muscle. She could feel blood dribbling, and the fox's growl vibrating against her bones. As it saw her fury, a crazed look came over its yellow eyes, and it bit down harder. Storm gasped. Blinking lights and patches of darkness danced in front of her eyes as the pain hit, eased off, and swelled again. "Mangy not-dogs! Get—*off!*"

She threw back her head and seized the creature's scruff in her teeth. The fox gave a yelp of pain and its jaws released their grip on her leg. Storm tossed the fox away from her, fury giving her a burst of extra strength, and it flew halfway across the clearing and plowed into one of its Packmates, knocking them both to the ground in a bloodied heap.

Storm's vision swam again. The blood trickling over her back paw was warm. She tried to shake her head, but it just made the shadows swimming in front of her bigger and darker.

Foxes charged toward her, and a rush of fury flowed through Storm. She roared and snapped at the creatures, feeling like she was falling into the dark, as if there were foxes clinging to her back and neck, slowing her down. Anger pulsed in her ears and throbbed in her head. Her skull felt too small to contain her rage. And then . . .

She wasn't sure where she was—her belly was flat on the ground. She could smell blood and leaf mulch and fox and dog, and she could hear a terrifying growl from somewhere nearby. Strong paws were holding her down. She writhed, trying to throw off her attacker, but she was too exhausted to move against the weight on her side.

"Storm!" The dog's voice was deep, familiar. It was Arrow. "Storm, stop. It's over."

The black cloud over Storm's eyes cleared away, and bit by bit she started to see the scene in front of her: Arrow's face, concerned but stern, looking into her own. The foxes, cowering back, vanishing into the thicket of thorns where the dogs couldn't follow. One of them struggling to keep up, hobbling on one hind leg, with the other hanging loose and bleeding.

And then the rest of the dogs. They should have been watching the foxes go, barking after them in triumph . . . but instead they were all staring at Arrow and Storm. Lucky's eyes were full of confusion and disbelief.

The other faces were full of fear.

CHAPTER ELEVEN

This is what happened before.

"Let me up," Storm managed to say, trying to keep her voice calm. Arrow hesitated. Storm didn't blame him.

This is what happened when Terror died.

Sometimes Storm thought that Lucky believed she had murdered the mad dog Alpha in cold blood, calculatedly, to free Twitch and his Pack from Terror's deranged rule. And sometimes she thought he believed she had given in to her Fierce Dog nature, let herself feel pleasure in sinking her teeth into another dog's throat. She knew it worried Lucky to think that she would be capable of something like that. But the truth was all those things . . . and none of them.

Storm didn't fully remember Terror's death.

BOOK 2: DEAD OF NIGHT

She remembered attacking Terror, remembered how she had fought against the mad dog and torn his jaw clean from his face. And she knew that he had died. But in between, there was a dark pit of uncertainty.

She hadn't been deprived of sleep back then—she had simply been furious. They had traveled all the way back to the Dog-Garden, in search of Fiery, Moon's lost mate, who had been kidnapped by the bad longpaws in the shiny yellow furs. All the way, Lucky had seemed worried that Storm—Lick, as she'd been back then—wouldn't be able to cope with seeing her old home again. He thought her Fierce Dog instincts would overwhelm her. And then, when she'd seen it . . . loudcages full of poisoned animals, Fiery wounded and sick, the Fierce Dog called Axe taking his revenge on the longpaws who had caged him and made him drink the bad river water . . .

Her fury had burned white hot inside her. She hadn't just been angry with the longpaws, or with Terror for enslaving his Pack through fear—she had been angry with the whole world. In her mind, she had raged against Earth-Dog herself, for bringing them so far and then letting Fiery die, even though they had managed to rescue him from his cage.

Perhaps Lucky had been right. Perhaps, when it had come to a fight against Terror, she really had succumbed to some Fierce Dog urge to rip and tear. . . .

To *kill* . . .

In the foxes' clearing, Arrow finally stood back, and Storm rolled onto her belly, feeling the pain in her hind leg as a distant throbbing.

She could see the same looks on the faces of the other dogs as she had seen on Lucky's when she had killed Terror.

They're not seeing the loyal Packmate who hunts with them every day. They're not even seeing the dog who defeated Blade on the ice and ended the Storm of Dogs.

All they see is a savage Fierce Dog.

And perhaps they were right. There was blood on her lips, and mud and scraps of red fur under her claws.

Storm dragged herself to her feet, her tail drooping. Without a word to the others, without even waiting for Lucky to say anything, she turned and squeezed through the gap in the nettles and out of the foxes' clearing.

Somewhere out in the forest she could hear the sound of running water, and it called to her with its promise of something cool and clean. She limped between the trees, trying not to put too much weight on her injured hind leg, until she found a stream that ran through the woods, trickling over a bed of smooth stones.

She walked into the water until it came about halfway up her legs, gasping when it hit her wound. She stood tense and still for a moment, until the chill started to numb the pain. Then she worked her paws against the gleaming stones, shuddering as mud and fur and trails of blood flowed away from her claws.

Whining, Storm lowered her head, and then plunged her muzzle into the cold water. It filled her nostrils and she opened her mouth, letting the water in, washing away the taste of fox blood that clung to her tongue. She rubbed her face against the stones, trying to get clean, not caring that she couldn't breathe. . . .

Something pushed against her shoulder and she raised her head, trailing drops of cold water—but it was only Mickey. He was standing in the stream too, his long black-and-white fur soaking wet and sticking to his legs. He pressed his head against her shoulder again and gently but firmly steered her back onto the bank. She didn't fight him.

"What are you thinking?" Mickey muttered. "You were under far too long. You'll drown yourself! What would Martha say if she saw you doing that?"

Hearing Martha's name was almost too much for Storm.

She whined and cringed away from Mickey. "I just wanted to get clean," she said, in a voice so quiet she could barely hear it herself. "I can feel the blood on me. . . ."

Mickey stepped forward and pressed his neck to Storm's, then gave her a sympathetic lick between her eyes. "I know. But you won't make it better by hurting yourself. Think, Storm. . . . If this is frightening for you, think how the others are feeling. Running off by yourself and coming back half-drowned isn't going to make them any less wary of you."

"I don't want them to be wary of me," Storm whined, feeling very small. "That's the point. I just wanted to make things better."

"And they will be," Mickey said. "As long as we can show them you're not afraid of yourself."

Storm looked up at him, unsure what to say. *But I am afraid of myself—at least, I'm not sure if I should be.*

"Now, come on," Mickey said briskly, kindly but commanding. "We need to get back to camp. You just keep a level head and don't let them see that you're worried," he added. "The others won't think anything of it. I promise."

His voice was so reassuring that Storm followed him, hopeful that he might be right. She couldn't feel the blood anymore—maybe she had washed it all off, after all. Maybe the other dogs wouldn't be afraid of her if she didn't let them think she was afraid.

Still, there was a nagging part of her that wouldn't be put down so easily.

If you can drive off a whole pack of foxes without knowing it, the voice said, *who's to say you couldn't kill one small gray dog in your sleep?*

"There they are!"

Storm heard Beetle's bark ring out from the camp and felt a burst of relief. Lucky gave a bark of triumph and broke into a run. Storm adjusted the rabbit she was carrying in her jaws and followed, lagging behind a little on her wounded hind leg, but just as glad to be home at last.

As soon as the dogs stepped into camp, they were surrounded by their Packmates, cheering for their safe return and clamoring to know whether they'd driven off the foxes.

"Give them space," said a voice, and Storm was happy to see Alpha coming toward them. Behind her, the four pups wriggled and sniffed curiously at the edge of their den. Lucky dropped his rabbit and bounded toward her, rubbing the side of his face along hers and licking her ears.

"I'm glad you're all safe," Bella said, though Storm noticed that her gaze lingered on Arrow. "It must have gone well—you brought prey!"

"The fight was so easy we still had energy to hunt on the way back," Snap said proudly, placing her rabbit with the others. The prey pile was looking impressive now. "Forest-Dog was good to us today. We'll eat well tonight!"

"It's over, Sweet," Lucky said quietly, leaning his head close to his mate. "They won't bother us again."

Storm frowned. She was sure they had scared the foxes away . . . for now. But the not-dogs had been more than willing to fight, and they would have had no idea that the Pack thought they were defending themselves—only that they came into the foxes' den and attacked.

She found herself meeting Arrow's eyes over the heads of the excited, triumphant dogs. He didn't look convinced either.

We've dealt with the foxes . . . but for how long?

CHAPTER TWELVE

Storm burst from the thicket and snapped at Fox Ash, forcing her back. The other dogs were somewhere close, leaping into the fray, snapping and snarling. Arrow scrambled over the fallen tree. The foxes yapped and backed away from him. Storm surged forward, and two of the foxes glared at her with fire in their eyes and leaped.

I've done this already, *Storm thought.* It's just a memory . . . nothing to worry about.

She felt a distant prickling of pain in her back as they latched on. Just as she had before, she bucked and threw them off. She felt much calmer than she had felt during the fight—this was a dream, so she didn't have to be afraid. The dogs had already won.

The third fox charged at her, and she brought her forepaw down across its muzzle. She saw the fox's head bounce on the hard ground, its ribs heaving, its eyes glazed, just like before. This time she knew it wasn't really stunned, but she still felt herself turning anyway, looking for other dogs to help.

No! she tried to tell herself. Turn back! It's going to—

In the dream, the bite on her hind leg felt distant, no worse than the scratch of a thorn. But her anger was sharper, clearer than the muzzled fury she'd felt in the real fight. Rage filled her body, until she thought she could tear down the whole world in vengeance—for herself, for Whisper, for the way the Pack treated Arrow, and the Fierce Dog's stoic silence. . . .

Storm threw back her head, seized the creature's scruff in her teeth, and threw it away from her. It flew halfway across the clearing and plowed into one of its Packmates, knocking them both to the ground.

More foxes charged, and Storm let her fury overwhelm and consume her. The part of her that was dreaming and aware expected the shadows to fall and the scene to go black. Storm expected to wake up. But she didn't.

Instead, this time, she saw everything.

She saw herself snap at one fox and then another. She smacked one to the ground and trod hard on its face, grinding it into the mud. She watched herself in horror as she leaped right into the middle of the group of foxes—a stupid thing to do, no matter how small the enemy. She could have been flanked and overwhelmed.

But she wasn't. Storm saw terror gleaming in the foxes' amber eyes as they cowered back from her raking claws, her slavering jaws and snapping teeth.

She saw, too, the unease in the eyes of the other dogs. Storm floated above herself, able to turn and see that her Packmates had stopped fighting. There were no foxes left for them to fight. Storm was taking on all the not-dogs herself, biting and snarling, while the other dogs backed away.

Storm felt the snap of a fox's leg in her jaws and heard its howl of anguish. She saw the foxes retreat and felt herself start to run after them. She hadn't finished with them yet. She wasn't going to be finished until they all lay still at her paws. . . .

Then there was a pressure against her flank, trying to push her down.

Arrow.

Except . . . no, this wasn't Arrow. It felt different. The paws were smaller, weaker. They were scrabbling gently, trying to get her attention. . . .

She turned her head, dream-dog and dreaming-dog moving together, and saw Whisper with his paws resting on her side. She flinched back, but he kept his paws on her. His eyes were still blank, clouded over with death, but there was a look on his face that was almost . . . friendly.

"Storm, no," he said. "You're better than this. You don't need to be so vicious. You're a Good Dog, a Brave Dog!"

Storm wanted to believe him more than anything in the world.

But then she felt another flood of rage, harsher than the first. How dare he keep saying that? How could he tell her she was a Good Dog, after what she had done?

She turned on Whisper, and he didn't resist as she knocked him to the ground and sank her teeth into his neck. . . .

* * *

Storm's paws ached with the cold, and for a moment she stared down at the water rushing by, thinking she was still dreaming. She had run to the stream, Whisper's blood still on her muzzle. Mickey would come and fetch her and perhaps she would kill him, too. . . .

But the ground under her paws was mud and sand, not hard stones, and she wasn't back in the foxes' territory. She was at the river, and she was awake now.

Storm recoiled, bounding back to the riverbank, trailing droplets after her. She shivered, looking around. She had wandered a long way. She was half-relieved that at least she'd left the camp and the other dogs far behind her, but even so, she felt disappointed with herself. How could she have let herself sleep deeply enough to dream? She'd thought she was getting so good at jerking herself awake before the darkness could take her. . . .

In fact, when had she gone to sleep at all? She stood and watched the river running by, trying not to let herself panic. She found herself listening out for howls of fear and grief, for a sign she might have done something terrible while the dream-Storm had been battling the foxes . . . and poor Whisper. . . .

She shook herself, flinging away drops of river water, and tried to focus. When had she last been in the den? What was the last thing a dog—a real dog—had said to her? It was something about a hunt. . . .

"There you are!"

Storm turned, almost tripping over her own paws in her surprise. It was Arrow. He pricked his pointed ears when he saw her wet fur.

"You must be eager to get going," he said, without any hint of fear in his voice. "But you can't hunt by yourself, you know. You have to wait for the rest of us."

That's right! Storm remembered in a flash. *I agreed to go on a hunt in the woods by the river—I just wanted to rest my eyes first. I must have remembered where I was supposed to go, despite myself.*

"I just wanted to wash my leg in some cool water," she said. It wasn't totally a lie—her wound was definitely feeling better than it had when she lay down.

Her relief redoubled when the dogs who joined Arrow at the top of the bank turned out to be Bella, Mickey, and Daisy—dogs who trusted her, who looked at her without that terrible unease in their eyes. They waited for her to scramble up to join them, but said nothing more about her journey to the river by herself, or any trouble back at camp.

It still wasn't a good sign that she had been sleepwalking, but at least she had walked to somewhere that she knew and had not hurt any dog along the way.

Bella was leading the hunting patrol, and Storm and the others followed her to a place where the trees stretched right down to the edge of the river, crowding thickly together. Storm remembered she had caught a large weasel here once, and she'd scented other creatures too, ones she wasn't quite familiar with. There would be no big, flashy kills like deer or tusknose here, but if they were lucky, they might catch many small treats for the Pack.

"Daisy, you go along the river and double back toward us," Bella ordered. "Try to scare any prey you find back this way. The rest of us will fan out and make our way through until we meet on the other side of the trees. Arrow, Storm, Mickey: Be ready to pounce on anything that moves."

Storm gave Bella a nod to signal that she'd understood, and then walked a little way along the tree line, leaving Bella closest to the riverbank, and Arrow between Bella and Storm. Mickey trotted past Storm to take up his position a rabbit-chase farther down, and at a signal from Bella, they all began to walk slowly into the shadow of the trees.

The day was dim and cool underneath the canopy of leaves. Storm was almost distracted from the hunt by how thick the branches were, and how green everything smelled. Whatever dog had called this season New Leaf had named it well—there were more leaves than she could ever count in a hundred seasons. She could hear birds up in the branches—small ones, twittering away to one another, far too high and fast for the dogs to catch.

She couldn't smell very much prey, though. In fact, she couldn't even smell Arrow or Mickey anymore. The trees grew so thickly here. Everything seemed so still.

Storm stopped and raised her head, sniffing. She could scent only what was right in front of her—the trees, the new leaves, and the odd hole where a prey-creature had made its den once, but wasn't there anymore. But it wasn't because those things smelled most strongly, it was because there was no breeze to carry other scents to her.

It's like the Wind-Dogs are . . . somewhere else. Not here.

She wondered if it was just this part of the wood, and what Alpha would say about a place where the Wind-Dogs were unable—or unwilling—to go.

And if it's not just here, if the Wind-Dogs have gone somewhere else . . . where would they go?

Perhaps they had chased the Golden Deer out of the Pack's territory . . . perhaps . . .

There was a low growl, and Storm's hackles rose for a moment before she realized that it was Arrow's voice she was hearing. She turned and picked her way through the trees toward the sound, until she could see Arrow's distinctive shape, and a flash of Bella's golden fur a few pawsteps farther on. She watched them carefully. Perhaps they'd want her help—or perhaps if she tried to help, she would disturb whatever prey they were stalking.

She stopped with her flank pressed to a tree, waiting to hear them whisper a plan or an order to each other that would tell her if she was needed.

But the two dogs said nothing. Arrow raised his head, and his ears flicked back for a second. Bella's tail wagged low to the ground, and she crouched. Arrow gave a jerk of his head, and Bella nodded, as if she'd understood him completely, and without having spoken a word to each other, the two dogs turned and separated.

A moment later, Storm heard a squeak—some small prey-creature had been caught unawares. Whatever their plan had been, it had worked.

Storm turned back to moving through the forest, but she

couldn't help thinking about what it would be like to know a dog who understood you so deeply you could strategize without speaking. It was amazing, really—but when Storm tried to imagine it, she only felt uncomfortable.

Storm stretched out on her back and looked up at the sky. The Sun-Dog was going to sleep, and the clouds above her were streaked with pink and yellow, parting here and there to show a glimpse of deep blue and glinting stars. In the distance, she could hear the constant soft sloshing of the Endless Lake and the cries of the big white lake birds.

The camp was peaceful. The Pack had eaten well, with a few rabbits still left over from their last meal and a bundle of smaller prey from this afternoon's hunt. The foxes were gone, and all the dogs seemed to have let go of their fear and anger, at least for the moment. Alpha and the pups were out of their den, lying in the warm evening air to be with their Packmates. Several of the dogs had gone over to say hello, pay their respects to Alpha, and play with the pups until they were tired out. Now the pups were lying in the soft curve of Alpha's body and listening to Lucky telling a story about the Spirit Dogs.

It was nice . . . though underneath the calm, Storm could feel the deep river of darkness still flowing, ready to flood over them all again. There was a killer in their midst, enjoying the peace with them, sharing their food and their warmth.

But even with that knowledge weighing heavily on her mind, Storm felt herself beginning to relax, just a little—the evening was so quiet, the world so still.

She made herself push the thoughts away, rolled over, and listened to Lucky instead.

"And I'm going to catch it," he was saying.

The pups were too young to talk, but they were old enough to listen, and they all looked completely enraptured by their father's words. They stared at Lucky as if he were the Forest-Dog himself.

"And once I catch the Golden Deer for you, the Wind-Dogs will bless you pups with good luck for your whole lives," Lucky went on. "You will always be safe, and the Spirit Dogs will always look after you."

"Dahs!" yapped Fluff, and tried to climb up on Lucky's paws, but she slipped and fell onto her back. Tiny laughed, a movement that seemed to shake her entire small body.

"Hello, Storm," said Arrow, padding up beside her.

Storm craned her neck to look at him and gave him a slow, satisfied blink. "Lucky's pups are nice, aren't they?"

The look on Arrow's face was like a cold drop of rain falling on Storm from a high-up branch. He glanced over at the pups, and his face tightened with worry.

"Can you come with me?" he asked.

Storm almost wanted to stay and hear more about how nothing bad would ever happen and the Spirit Dogs would protect the Pack for the rest of their lives. But instead she reluctantly stood up and followed him.

Arrow led her past the Patrol Dogs' den and around the tree behind it, but instead of going farther out of camp, he stopped right next to the bone pile. Storm looked down at the pile of inedible, chewed-up remains of prey, and her stomach turned just a little.

"What's the matter?" she asked. "Why are we here?"

"I don't dare take this to Alpha, because I'm afraid she'll think I'm making things up." Arrow stared at the bones, deep in thought. "It's just . . . did you think there was something strange about the prey tonight? Something that was just . . . a bit *off*?"

Storm thought back to the meal, but she didn't have to rack her brains too hard—it had seemed completely ordinary. "Not as tasty as some meals we've had, I suppose," she said. "But I thought it was just because some of those small prey-creatures that we catch in the woods are skinny and tough. Not much meat on their bones."

Arrow gave a huff and shook his head. "That's what Bella said."

"Well," Storm said, as gently as she could, "perhaps she was right. I know that we both know that—that not everything is as well as it seems," she added darkly. "But perhaps, this time, you're chasing your own shadow."

"No." Arrow shook his head and pawed at the edge of the bone pile in frustration. "No, I know what I smelled and tasted. There was something wrong with it. It tasted *foul*. And then I found this." He nudged aside a pile of bones, picked clean and chewed up. As he did so, a smell hit Storm's nose, and she recoiled.

There *was* something foul there—and fouler than normal for the bone pile.

She forced herself to look.

It was a rat. Not the chewed remains of a fresh rat—a whole, uneaten, moldy rat. It was green and stinking, rotted through. Flies crawled through its fur.

"What—what is that doing there?" Storm managed, not wanting to breathe in too close to the stinking thing. "Who would put a whole rat in the bone pile?"

"I don't know—but I don't think it was there yesterday." Arrow kneaded the ground uneasily. "The food tasted strange tonight, so I came here to see if I could find anything that might have made the prey taste wrong, and . . ."

"You think that was in the prey pile? The pile we all ate from?" Storm whined.

"I'm afraid so," Arrow said. "You and Bella might not have tasted it—it's small, so perhaps it would only have affected the prey it was touching. But if some dog could slip it into the pile and get it out again without being seen, then yes, I'm fairly sure at least one dog has eaten tainted prey tonight. I tasted it and stopped eating, but no other dog seems to have done the same."

Storm stared at him. She didn't know what to say—except to ask *why* again and again. She turned away so she wouldn't have to look at the festering rat in the bone pile.

Some dogs might get sick . . . and Arrow was right, it *must* have been done on purpose, or else whoever found the rat would have called out to the others instead of hiding it away in the bone pile, and every dog would know. A rotten piece of prey in the pile might have been a mistake, but hiding it away afterward . . . that was deliberate.

Dread filled Storm's heart, and fury that any dog would attack their Pack like this. . . .

And then, suddenly, a burst of relief so strong she almost wanted to howl. If this was all true, then they had a traitor in the camp, a dog who wasn't Storm.

I still don't know for certain what happened that night. I still don't know everything I do when I sleepwalk or when I let my rage get the better of me. But there is one thing I know for certain.

I did not do this!

She turned back to Arrow, unable to hide the energy that she suddenly felt in her paws. "Who can we tell? Who will believe us?"

Before Arrow could answer, a howl went up from the camp behind them, and then another joined it, discordant and anxious. Storm and Arrow shot brief glances at each other, then turned and bolted back past the patrol den.

"Stand back," Twitch's voice said. "Give her a little space. Bella? Bella, it's going to be all right."

"No . . . Bella!" Arrow barked, skidding to a halt in between Mickey and Snap. Storm hurried up to them and looked down at the golden dog—she was lying on the ground, her flanks heaving, her eyes rolling back in her head.

"Is she sick?" Storm asked, a terrible shudder running the length of her body, all her relief forgotten.

"Stand back, Storm," Twitch barked back. "She needs air."

Bella coughed, and her whole body seemed to ripple and shake for a moment. She rolled over, onto her paws, and got up. At once, Arrow bounded to her side and let her lean on him.

"Bella?" he whined softly. "O Earth-Dog, please be all right. . . ."

Storm worried that it might not be the best thing for Bella to stand, but the golden dog leaned on her mate for a moment, and her legs seemed to steady.

Then her chest heaved and she coughed up a stream of foul-smelling prey pieces. Most of the dogs backed away with horrified whines, their ears pressed back against their skulls. Bella kept on bringing up more and more hot, foul liquid, and even after it seemed there was nothing left inside her, she still coughed and retched, swaying weakly. Arrow looked up, casting a desperate gaze around at the other dogs. His anxious whine made some of them flinch, and others look at one another in horror.

"What can I do?" he begged. "Help her!"

CHAPTER THIRTEEN

Storm woke up in her own den, feeling the weight of sleeplessness lightly on her shoulders. She had made sure she didn't sleep through the night, so she wasn't fully rested—but these days, she barely remembered what that felt like. Instead she felt the comfortable sense of workable tiredness that she was starting to get very used to, and knew that it was time to get up, to walk around so her legs would remember how.

She was just glad that she wasn't sick.

Out in the camp, the smell of the sickness still lingered. It had been two journeys of the Sun-Dog since Arrow had spotted the rotting rat and Bella had started to throw up chunks of prey.

It had been a very long night. It wasn't just Bella—Twitch, Moon, and Woody had fallen sick too. All night, Storm and the other healthy dogs had run to the pond and back to bring cool reeds and moss soaked in water, like an entire Pack of Omegas. Which was fitting, Storm thought, because Sunshine herself had sickened after the Sun-Dog had finished his run. Finally Thorn had joined them the next morning, with great reluctance and grouchiness, as if she had been holding out as long as she could, refusing to let the sickness that was festering in her gut take her down as it had the others.

And yet, although it had been horrible, if the bad dog had intended to really hurt the Pack, then that plan had failed. The sickness didn't seem to have permanently harmed any of its victims. They were mostly lying out in the sun when Storm came out of the den, eating scraps of prey brought to them by Ruff and Daisy, or sleeping off the exhaustion.

Storm stretched her legs and shook herself to cast off the last of her sleep.

The Pack was still recovering, and Storm felt like she was too, in a way. She hadn't told Alpha or Beta what Arrow had suspected about the prey pile and the rotting rat, and neither had he. Was it too late now? Maybe it was too soon. She didn't want to panic the dogs while they were still getting better—and she especially didn't want any dog's suspicion to fall on her or Arrow. But at the same time, if some dog had poisoned the prey pile, then they were all in danger. . . .

Storm saw Lucky and Alpha near the entrance to their den, Lucky walking back and forth in a tight circle around his mate and their pups, who were curled up together between Alpha's paws.

Could Storm tell him? Should she?

Lucky caught Storm's eye, and Storm almost looked away, but Lucky called her over.

"Storm, come here a minute."

Storm tried to ignore her uneasy feeling at being summoned, and trotted over to Alpha's den.

"You haven't really met the pups yet, have you?" Lucky asked, with a kindly tilt of his head, when Storm got a little closer.

"Well . . . I *was* at the Den Break," Storm reminded him, wondering if he had forgotten.

Lucky shook his head. "I mean, just you and them. Come on, come and say hello."

Storm slowly padded closer to Alpha, suddenly nervous. She wasn't sure why—the pups were barely bigger than her paw, basically just fuzz with eyes. She stood beside Alpha, and those four pairs of eyes opened and stared up at her, wonder and awe mingling in their tiny depths. But then, suddenly, the balls of fuzz whined and pressed themselves close to their Mother-Dog.

Storm froze, not sure what to do, or what she'd done to frighten the pups. She must look huge to them—monstrous, even. Should she lick them? Or would that be terrifying to such small creatures? Would they whine and yowl? Would Lucky and Alpha hurry her away, before she scared their pups any further?

Martha would have known what to do.

Storm stepped back, sorrow biting deep in her chest. Martha would have known how to handle the pups, to make them like her, not to scare them—but Martha wasn't here anymore. She had been killed by Blade's Pack, defending Storm and the other dogs, and died lying in the snow on the edge of the frozen river.

Storm's fur bristled at the memory, and she knew at once that she had made things worse—the pups whined uneasily, looking to their Mother-Dog for reassurance. Storm backed off.

"I'm sorry," she muttered. "I—I should go. Sorry." She turned to leave.

"Storm," Alpha barked after her, "it's all right. They will get used to you in time."

Storm's ears twitched in acknowledgment, but she didn't turn back.

She made herself walk away slowly, resisting the urge to run or slink, her head buzzing with regrets . . . she should have been better with the pups, and she should have stayed farther away, and maybe she shouldn't have gone over there in the first place. . . .

"Storm, wait." Lucky appeared at her side and kept pace with her. "Are you all right?"

Storm hesitated, not sure what she could tell him. That she was afraid that she couldn't be near his pups? That was ridiculous. . . .

"You know," Lucky said, "I haven't been around very much recently—looking after the pups, taking care of the Pack while Alpha's nursing. But I will always be here for you. You're such a strong dog now, you don't need me like the pups do."

Storm couldn't think what to say—she felt touched, but guilty. Perhaps it was better for Lucky to think that she was jealous of the pups, instead of afraid that she would always be terrifying to them.

"Thank you, Beta," she said eventually. "I'll try to remember that."

No dog had felt very hungry the previous day—even the healthy dogs had been put off their food by the dire condition of their sick Packmates. But now there were a lot of empty bellies to fill, and some of them were starting to growl with hunger, including

Storm's. She was happy to join the hunting party that went out as the Sun-Dog was rising directly above them, and she was quite pleased to see that Lucky himself was leading it.

Mickey and Snap were with them, with Twitch and Dart acting as scout dogs. Twitch wasn't as fast on his three legs as some of the Patrol Dogs, but Storm was always glad to have him along. He always seemed to know good ways to trick and trap their prey into running to them, using his quick brain as much as his paws and teeth.

As they trotted across the meadow and between the trees, Mickey drew level with Lucky and caught his attention with a flick of his black-and-white tail.

"Beta, I've been thinking about the sickness," he said. Storm's heart beat a little faster, and she put on a small burst of speed, just enough that she could hear their conversation clearly. Had Mickey found the rat, or worked out that the prey had been tampered with?

"What about it?" Lucky asked.

"Well, it must have come from the prey," Mickey said. "It struck so suddenly, and only a few of us, and it was over so fast—it must have been a bad vole, or something like that. Perhaps there's a sickness in the forest!"

"Yes, you might be right," Lucky said. "But none of the prey *looked* sick—how can we tell if it's safe?"

"I wondered if we should hunt near the river," Mickey said. "Prey that lives near the water might be cleaner, and might not get sick."

"We could find a fish or two in the water," Snap added, from behind them. "Fish are good prey, if you can catch them."

Lucky was silent for a moment, then he shook his head. "Perhaps another day. For now, I think it's important we revisit our normal hunting places."

Snap's head twitched to the side. "Why? If you don't mind me asking, Beta," she added quickly.

Lucky exchanged a glance with Twitch.

"Some of the Patrol Dogs scented foxes and coyotes," he said finally. "Not in large numbers. We don't think they are making their camp near here. But even a *hint* of those creatures is enough. I don't want them thinking we've given up our territory. If they try to return and hunt where we hunt, then we'll end up fighting for every scrap. We need to make sure they know whose land this is."

"It's true . . ." Twitch said, although something about his tone made Storm think he wasn't quite so sure. "Some of the Patrol Dogs have reported fox-scents, but after the way you put the fear of Lightning into them before, I can't imagine they'll want to risk tangling with us again." He hesitated, but then went on. "Beta, I know what you seek. And I think that . . . *broader* hunting will be in the best interests of the Pack."

For a moment, Storm wasn't sure what Twitch meant—but then she thought back to the pups, and the story that Lucky had been telling them before Bella got sick.

Of course—the Golden Deer! He's still hoping to find it, and he wants to go back to where we saw it last . . . even though that might not be best for the whole Pack.

"After all, Alpha needs safe prey to eat—she needs that more than any of us, since she's feeding the pups," Twitch went on. Storm panted quietly, waiting to see how far Twitch would push his advice, and how Lucky would react. He was a good and sensible Beta, but he did not like being told what to do by any dog.

Lucky looked up at the sky for a moment, and then his ears twitched and he returned the Third Dog's gaze steadily. "Yes, that's true. You're right, Twitch. Let's see what the River-Dog has to offer. It's more important that we feed the Pack safely. We can search the forest another time."

Storm huffed to herself, pleased with Lucky's decision, as the dogs turned and veered toward the river.

163

* * *

Dart leaned over the bank, sniffing disdainfully at the water. "All I can see is myself," she said. "There might be fish in there, but the Sun-Dog is in the way. I wish he'd hurry and run behind the clouds so I could see."

For once, Storm completely agreed with Dart. She paced along the shore, twisting and turning her head, trying to spot the fish that she was sure were swimming underneath the surface, but the light glinting on the water was making it hard. The problem with fish was that there was no way to scent them until you already had them in your jaws.

"Even if we find the fish," she said quietly, "I'm not sure how we can catch them—surely if you tried to bite one, it would swim away and you'd just end up with a mouthful of river."

"I've seen it done," Snap said, but she was pawing the edge of the water a little uncertainly herself. "You have to be quick."

A low growl came from a little way upstream, and Storm looked over to see Twitch crouching on a rock that stuck out over the water, looking down. "I see one coming," he muttered. "It's swimming very close to the surface! Maybe we can get it."

At once, every dog stopped their complaining and went to the edge of the water, waiting for the fish to get close.

"If I miss it," Lucky muttered to Mickey, "it may panic, but it'll come straight toward you. We can each try, if the previous dogs don't catch it."

"Here it comes," Twitch barked, and Storm strained to see upriver. Would it be a large fish, big enough to feed many of the Pack? Or were they all risking a soaking for some darting little silver thing?

She saw it, suddenly—at first a different texture bobbing on top of the water, then a brownish color where the river current broke around its back.

It passed Lucky . . . and he didn't pounce. Neither did Mickey, or Twitch. They sat back and watched it go. Storm was about to bark a question, when the fish came closer, and she could see why it was swimming so slowly, so close to the surface.

It wasn't swimming at all. And it wasn't a fish.

Deep wounds scored its flanks, and its upturned eye was blank and staring. It was a rabbit, and it was dead.

"Who would kill a creature and then just leave it in the water?" she said, disgusted at the idea of rotting prey sitting in the water that the Pack sometimes drank from. "That's an insult to the River-Dog!"

"River is river, dog is dog, no silly spirits, no help coming," said a sneering voice, and at the same time Storm's nose picked up a familiar, horrible scent. "Turn and face us, dogs."

The dogs spun around, snarling, to find a pack of coyotes lined up on the riverbank behind them.

CHAPTER FOURTEEN

"This is your doing, then," Lucky growled. He stepped forward, and the other dogs lined up loyally behind him, fixing the coyotes with their angriest stares. Storm counted eight coyotes, including one with a missing tail. There were six dogs in the hunting party.

Six dogs can take eight coyotes any day, she thought, and felt better for it—but only slightly.

"Why would you leave prey in the river?" Lucky snapped. "Are you trying to offend the River-Dog?"

"No silly spirits," said the coyotes' leader smugly, tossing his head back and baring his teeth. "Not like foolish dogs. We see what is in front."

Storm suppressed a shudder. She didn't want to look weak in front of the coyotes, but her skin was crawling underneath her fur. If the coyotes did this intentionally, trying to poison the

River-Dog, was it possible that *they* could have been responsible for the rat in the Pack's prey pile?

But no—there was no way the coyotes could have gotten close enough. Even several paw strides away, she could smell their stink and almost see the fleas leaping around in their fur. They could never have planted the rat without being spotted, let alone cleared it away again.

That meant it had to be a dog in the Pack.

Before she could get caught up again in wondering who—and *why*—Lucky stepped forward, his head high and his teeth bared.

"If it's a fight you mangy creatures want, I warn you—every dog here is worth two of you, and we will give you a fight you will never forget!"

"Even *that* cripple?" The coyote leader sneered at Twitch. The coyotes behind him sniggered unpleasantly. "Twice a coyote? He's not even a whole dog!"

"*Especially* 'that cripple.'" Twitch walked forward, easy and confident on his three legs, and looked the coyote leader right in the eye. "Do you want to know how I lost my leg?" Twitch said, so quietly the coyotes were forced to stop laughing to hear him. "It was weak. No use to me. One day I got injured, and sick, and I was all alone. So I *chewed it off.* I walk, run, and fight better without it—and if you don't believe me, by all means, go ahead . . . try attacking me."

"Lie dog," the coyote leader muttered, but he looked at Twitch as if he were a rabbit who'd turned around and bitten him.

"I'd run, if I were you," Lucky said. "And if you have any sense, you had better leave this territory for good, and never let me see or scent you around here again. If I do, I'll let Twitch feed you to the Earth-Dog!"

"Earth is earth," the coyote leader snarled petulantly. For a moment longer, he stared at Lucky over Twitch's head. Then he bared his teeth mockingly at Twitch, turned, and bounded away, his coyote pack following him at a loping, sideways run so they could throw growls back over their shoulders at the dogs.

"Yeah, you'd better run away, mangy not-dogs," Dart muttered.

The dogs stood firm and watched the coyotes as they vanished into the trees, and as soon as they were out of earshot, Lucky heaved a deep sigh.

"That was close," he said.

"We should get back to camp and tell Alpha about this," Mickey suggested. "I hope we never see those coyotes again, but the Pack should know that they were out here, insulting the

River-Dog with their disgusting ways. I bet it was them that made the forest prey sick," he added.

I wish it was, Storm thought. *If only our enemy was an outsider like the coyotes. Things would be so much simpler.*

"Yes, let's get back. We can stop to hunt in one of the meadows on the way. The Pack will have enough, for the moment." Lucky shook himself, and then turned to the Third Dog. "Well done, Twitch! I think you frightened them more than I ever could."

All the quiet ferocity went out of Twitch, and he shook his head. "You know a lot of it was just a bluff, don't you? If they'd really attacked—well, I would have done my best, but . . ."

"Your best would have been good enough," Lucky told him firmly, as they started back up the bank and turned to follow the quickest path up to the Pack camp. "And what's really important is that the coyotes *didn't* know you were bluffing."

The dogs did manage to catch a few pieces of prey on their way back to the camp—it was barely enough for a single meager meal, but Storm was glad when Lucky announced it was time to go back. Some of their Packmates were unable to hide their disappointment, Bella in particular, but when Lucky reminded her that they had had coyotes and a potentially sick River-Dog to contend with, his litter-sister immediately changed her mind, declaring to the rest that it was practically a feast, and she wasn't that hungry anyway.

Storm watched the prey carefully as each dog approached, ate their fill—or slightly less than their fill—and then backed away again. She couldn't see any swarming flies or strangely slick fur among the prey. Every piece of prey seemed fine—but how could she know for certain what some dogs might be capable of doing?

Finally, after Sunshine had settled down to crunch the left-over bones and suck out the tasty marrow, the dogs lay down to rest, and Storm saw Twitch walk over to Alpha's den, his head bowed. He must be reporting to her about the coyotes—Storm guessed Lucky would have given her the brief version as soon as they got back, but now it was time for Alpha to hear the story in full and decide what they should do about it.

Storm carefully lay down, stretched, and rolled until she was close enough to Alpha's den to see and hear what was being discussed. She knew it was wrong for a young hunter to presume to listen in on her Alpha's conversation—but she assured herself it was no mere flash of curiosity. She needed to know what they were saying, because she was the only one who could clearly see the danger the Pack faced.

Alpha was lying with the pups curled against her side, fast asleep after a good feeding. Storm was quite relieved—she didn't think this was a conversation pups so small should hear, although she supposed at least they wouldn't know what a coyote was, or why they should be afraid of it.

I wish that was still true for me, she thought sadly. *I wish I'd never had to learn what a coyote was.*

"Thank you for telling me, Twitch," Alpha said solemnly. "You did the right thing—I don't want our dogs to have to fight for their lives every time they leave the camp. Those coyotes need to remember whose territory this is." She glanced down at her pups, and a gentle look came over her long face, but when she looked up at Lucky and Twitch again, it changed to one of strain and worry. "The Pack is getting bigger. Twitch's dogs, our dogs, the pups. More dogs are going to start taking mates and having their own pups. This territory is big enough for us now, but we might have to expand one day. I don't want us giving an inch to those creatures, not when the future of our Pack might be at stake."

Storm stared at her paws as she listened to Alpha's words. She had never thought of that—the future of the next generation seemed an impossibly long way away, but it wasn't. Mickey and Snap, Bella and Arrow—and who knew how many other pairs of mates she hadn't noticed?—they might have pups, and suddenly the Pack would need to find food and den space for five more dogs, or ten, or maybe even more.

More pups would be good—more pups means more hunters and more Patrol Dogs, more safety and more food. But it would also mean more mouths to feed. And if Bella and Snap couldn't hunt for a season, we would struggle. . . .

It was such a complex thought, the kind of thing that an Alpha had to deal with that no other dog would even consider. Storm felt a rush of admiration for the swift-dog, for her mind that could run as fast as her paws.

"That kind of Pack might be hard to keep . . . well organized," said Lucky. "If we're to make sure no creature thinks of taking us on, we have to seem like an intimidating force, and the more dogs we have, the harder it will be to keep control."

"We have to try," Alpha said firmly. "I think this is our fate, Lucky—to live here and grow our Pack. That's what the Spirit Dogs want for us. We must become stronger, not weaker, until it's impossible for any other dog to suffer as Whisper did."

Storm's ears twitched at the mention of the gray dog.

"Poor Whisper," Twitch muttered.

"He was such a good dog," Lucky agreed. "So eager to please. It's cruel for a dog like that to have been taken from us."

"Whisper always had a good heart," Twitch said. "When I was a Lone Dog out in the forest, I'd just lost my leg and I was desperate for a Pack, something to belong to . . . I found Terror's Pack, and I thought he was going to kill me on the spot. He even had the others baying for my blood. But Whisper talked him down."

Storm's ears pricked up at this. She'd always had the impression that Whisper was too scared of Terror to even breathe in his presence, let alone convince him to spare a dog's life!

"How did he manage that?" Alpha asked, echoing Storm's thoughts.

"He told Terror I would be more . . . amusing . . . to keep in the Pack for a while. After a few days, I'd proved myself capable, and I think Terror forgot all about my leg. He just saw me as another one of his Pack, another dog to manipulate and frighten. It was a bad life. But it was a *life*, and I owed it all to Whisper."

"I wish the pups had waited a few more days to come," Alpha said. "I was glad to meet them, of course, but I feel as if I never had the chance to mourn Whisper properly. I wish I'd known him longer, and better. He was a Good Dog."

Storm rolled over onto her side and squeezed her eyes shut. Her heart ached, like the slowly healing wound in her hind leg.

I still don't know for certain how he died—or what things I do after I've fallen asleep. I have to get to the bottom of all this, but until I do, I won't let myself put the other dogs in danger.

She sat up straight, dragging herself away from her position of comfort and forcing her eyes open.

I mustn't sleep too deeply. I must get to the truth.

I owe Whisper that much.

CHAPTER FIFTEEN

Storm sat up on her hind legs, leaning against the trunk of a tree at the edge of the camp, and watched the sky get lighter and lighter. The Sun-Dog would begin his journey across the sky any minute, and Storm would be waiting to greet him, just like she had been the previous day, and the one before.

She could hear dogs starting to stir in their dens—the hunters scrabbling and the Patrol Dogs snuffling, and even the faint squeaking yaps of the four pups. Down by the pond, three dark shapes moved against the bright grass, coming toward the camp. For a moment, though she knew that they were dogs, Storm couldn't pick out their individual shapes. Then she blinked and the fog in front of her eyes cleared, and she could see that the dogs were Daisy, Thorn, and Beetle.

"Good morning," Daisy panted, as they trotted past Storm

and into the camp. "You're up early." She cocked her head just slightly as she said it, one ear lifting in curiosity.

"It's a lovely morning," Storm said, and gave Daisy what she hoped was a reassuring blink. *It's all right. I haven't been sleepwalking.*

Daisy seemed to accept this and followed the others into the camp with her tail wagging.

"Let's eat," she said to the other two, "and then I'm going straight to the den."

Storm turned to watch the Patrol Dogs as they approached the prey pile and began to pick out their ration of leftovers from the previous night. They would take enough to replenish their strength, and the rest would be shared between the other dogs when they awoke. In fact, she could see the new patrol getting up, stretching, and preparing to leave the camp—Breeze, Ruff, and Rake would be going out next. They stood close to the three night Patrol Dogs, but they didn't speak, not even to ask if there was anything to report, or to say good morning.

Strange, Storm thought, as she watched them. *I never noticed before . . . Alpha's Pack and Twitch's Pack don't really talk very much. It's not that they're snapping or growling at one another. They're all good dogs—they're just not talking.*

She knew that sometimes when the Packs worked together,

arguments broke out—especially after Whisper's death—but surely it couldn't be a good idea to let the patrols split themselves up like this?

Does Alpha know? Should I tell her?

No, that was a foolish idea. Storm stretched out, arching her back until it gave a satisfying crunch. *Nobody asked my opinion. I'm sure it'll be fine.*

The sky grew even brighter, and Storm found herself blinking more and more, trying to clear the strange gritty texture from the corners of her eyes. Her paws felt hot and sore—she had gone hunting yesterday, and despite her exhaustion she had felt more alive than ever, pounding over the grass as if the Wind-Dogs were with her. Keeping herself awake last night had been hard, but the wobbly feeling in her legs was almost pleasant when it came with such an intense feeling of triumph.

Storm had stayed awake for two days and two nights, except for snatched moments of sleep here and there, and she hadn't gone walking in her dreams, or done *anything* without being aware of it. She felt as if she was perfectly in control of herself, *contained* somehow, almost as if the rest of the world could not even touch her.

She felt a rumble in her stomach, stretched again, and headed for the prey pile. *I haven't been out patrolling all night,* she thought, *but*

I've been protecting the Pack, in my own way.

Daisy, Thorn, and Beetle had finished eating and gone into the patrol den. As Storm passed the shady, enclosed space she could hear the scuffling of their pawsteps as they trod their sleep circles, ready to settle down. She felt a small pang of envy, but put it out of her mind. She didn't need sleep—she just needed something to eat, and she would be fine. . . .

The Sun-Dog was rising and the light was changing, even as she walked across the camp toward the leftover prey. The great bright dog leaped into the sky, and the streams of light and shadow leaped with him. Between the trees, the sharp light and deep black shifted around, and Storm saw . . . a dog.

A dog who could not be there.

She was tall and sleek, her pointed black ears like shards of broken clear-stone. Her eyes were points of light that held Storm frozen to the spot with dread.

It can't be. Blade is dead!

But Storm could *see* her, could see her eyes blinking, her dark shape outlined against the shifting patterns of light between the trees. Storm's stomach churned and the camp seemed to tip up under her paws, almost like a new Growl of the Earth-Dog. . . .

And then she blinked and Blade was gone, and the Earth-Dog

was still once more. Storm stared into the trees, panting fast, her chest tight with worry. But there was nothing there.

"Storm, are you all right?" some dog barked, and Storm forced herself to tear her gaze away from the spot where she had seen—had thought she'd seen—the Fierce Dog Alpha. Snap looked from Storm to the trees, and Storm could see in the small female's eyes that she wasn't seeing anything out of the ordinary.

"Yes, fine. Just thinking. Sorry." *It was the Sun-Dog playing tricks on me*, Storm thought, looking away. *That's all. He knows I've been thinking about Fierce Dogs and bad dogs, and he tried to scare me. But it won't work.*

Blade was dead, defeated by Storm and her Packmates, drowned in the frozen river.

Storm went to the prey pile and sniffed among the scraps, her teeth almost closing on the remains of a scrawny squirrel, when she smelled something that made her recoil, blinking hard.

"Yuck!" she whined. "What is that?"

Something was wrong here. Something rotten was in the prey pile.

It was happening again.

She tried to fight back the urge to panic. *Maybe whoever did it last time didn't think we got sick enough. Maybe they want the whole Pack to go down. To weaken us . . . or kill some dog.*

Storm forced herself to lean forward again, to nose at the prey, turning over the squirrel and the piece of mouse underneath it. The smell grew stronger as she dug down, but she couldn't find any rotten prey like the rat that was buried last time—there was just something *wrong*. The smell was sweet and sickly and foul all at the same time, and it was all over the prey she'd been just about to gobble down.

We didn't tell any dog, she thought, stepping back, her vision swimming for a second. *We didn't tell anyone about the rat, and now it's happened again. Stupid! We should have told the whole Pack. Why didn't I think that this might happen?*

She was backing off, sniffing hard, trying to clear the smell from her muzzle so that she could run to the bone pile and search for the bad prey that had done this, when her hind legs struck something soft, and she stumbled.

"Watch out, Storm," said Lucky kindly. "With those big paws of yours, you could tread a smaller dog into the ground—" His eyes met hers and he stopped. "Storm, what is it?"

"The prey . . ." Storm whined. "There's something wrong with it."

Lucky stepped forward and sniffed the prey pile, recoiling with a shudder. "What is that?"

"Something rotten," Storm answered, without thinking. Before she could say any more, a plaintive whine split the air. It was coming from the Patrol Dogs' den. Storm spun around and bounded the few steps from the prey pile to the den just in time to see Daisy step outside on unsteady paws. She looked up at Storm with huge, watery eyes.

"Oh, Storm . . . I don't feel well at all. . . ."

Storm could see that she was sick. The little white dog was panting hard, and her ears couldn't seem to keep still. She was twitching from nose to tail.

"What's going on?" said Bella's voice, hollow with fear. "Is it—is it back? The sickness?" Storm looked over her shoulder and found the other Pack Dogs starting to gather around, worry and disgust in their faces.

"There's something bad in the food," Lucky said. He turned to face the other dogs, standing between them and the prey pile. "Be careful, stand back."

"It must be from yesterday's hunt," Bruno muttered. His voice rose as he went on. "The hunting party must have brought back prey that was sick. Why didn't any dog smell it? Who knows how many of us might get sick this time?"

Storm bristled at his accusing tone. *That's just what a dog would say if they had planted the bad prey here.* She stopped herself from saying it just in time. It wouldn't help Daisy for her to start throwing accusations around too. Instead she looked at Lucky, willing him to respond. He had been on the hunt along with her, and Mickey, and Twitch. . . .

"No, we would have scented it," Twitch said firmly. "We've been so careful—after the last time, we've been keeping alert for signs of sickness. We checked it all, and it was good prey."

"Twitch is right," Lucky agreed. "Nothing we brought back yesterday smelled like this does."

Bruno still seemed dissatisfied. His ear flicked and he looked right at Storm. "Maybe *some dog* wasn't as careful as the rest of you," he said.

Mickey let out a low growl, his black-and-white tail swishing low against the ground. "If something was wrong with the prey we brought last night, why aren't we all sick now? Why didn't any of us smell this? Some sick creature must have crawled into the prey pile and died overnight," he added. "That's the only way it could have gone this bad this fast."

It's not the only way. Storm looked for Arrow in the crowd of anxious dogs. He was standing beside Bella, steadying her as she kneaded the ground with her paws, but his eyes were searching the faces of the dogs nearby. They finally fell on Storm's.

What can we say? What will the others say if we come out with our suspicion now—that there's a bad dog in the camp, sabotaging our food?

Lucky had scolded her like a puppy when she had tried to suggest that a dog killed Whisper. Even when the Pack had listened to her ideas and discussed them, they seemed to have dismissed them.

If I try to tell them, they'll just call me a troublemaker . . . and if Arrow says something, they might just turn on him and say he did it himself.

Daisy whimpered again, and Storm turned away from Arrow and the other dogs and bent her head to the small, sick dog, giving her a soft, tentative lick on the ear.

"I think I'm sick too," said Thorn, who had come to the entrance of the patrol den but couldn't seem to walk any farther. She lay down, with her nose just poking out into the sunshine. "I feel so . . . weak. . . ."

Moon scrambled past the others, past Lucky and Storm, to lie down with her muzzle beside her sick pup's. "It's all right," she murmured. "You're going to be all right. Beetle, are you in there?"

Thorn's litter-brother took a few hesitant steps out of the patrol den, but he didn't seem stiff or dizzy—just frightened.

"I'm here," he said. "I don't feel sick."

"Beetle, did you eat after you came in from the hunt?" Storm asked urgently.

"No," Beetle said, in a small voice. "I wasn't hungry. . . . Daisy and Thorn were both hungry, but I wasn't, and now . . ."

"You see?" Mickey snapped, turning to Bruno. "It was only the morning prey that was sick!"

"It doesn't matter now," Lucky said, though Storm didn't think that he sounded entirely convinced about that. "We can't stand here arguing about it! Mickey, Dart, take all the prey—*carefully*—and bury it. Not in the bone pile—somewhere far away from camp."

"Yes, Beta," said Mickey, and bravely stepped forward to pick up the bad food in his jaws. Dart came a little more hesitantly, her flanks shuddering and her tail between her legs, but she picked up the remains of the mouse and followed Mickey out of the camp at a scrabbling run.

"I'll take another hunting party out right away," Lucky said, "to replenish the prey pile. And we'll move it, in case the sickness is in the ground on this spot. Bruno, you can join me—perhaps then you'll believe that we've checked the prey properly," he added, with an edge in his voice.

Bruno stood up straight, but his ears twisted back at the same time, and he couldn't quite meet his Beta's eyes. Storm was comforted to see that he at least seemed a little bit ashamed.

Lucky looked around at the other dogs. "Bella, if you're up to it, and Snap, why don't you come too? We'll take Twitch as our scout dog."

Storm waited to hear her name, but Lucky didn't go on. She blinked, surprised and disappointed. Her aching paws itched to go for a run, to get her heart beating and stamp down the rising tide of exhaustion that lapped at her legs all the time now. "Beta, don't you want to bring a few more hunters?" she asked. "I could—"

"No, Storm," said Lucky. Storm cocked one ear—Lucky hadn't even let her get her request out before he'd cut her off. "I want you to go down to the river and gather the long grasses that grow there—Moon says they helped settle the sick dogs' stomachs last time."

"Grasses?" For a moment, Storm wasn't sure she had heard him right—she heard a buzzing noise in her ears, like an angry fly had landed on top of her head. It wasn't that she minded helping Sunshine out with her chores, when it was needed—but surely Lucky had made a mistake? "But I can hunt, and Omega—"

"Omega will have plenty to do tending to Daisy and Thorn,"

Lucky said sternly. "More to the point, I don't want to send her to the river. Not when I can't guarantee she'll be safe from the foxes or the coyotes. *You* can look after yourself."

Storm dipped her head in understanding. It wasn't the same as catching prey, following their delicious scents across the meadows and through the forests until she could outrun or outwit them, killing them with a quick, clean bite to the throat . . . but it would mean a run down to the river, at least.

The hunting party gathered, and the rest of the dogs started to split up and wander away, either joining their sick Pack-mates or crawling back to their dens. Storm gave Daisy another encouraging nudge with her muzzle, and when she looked up, Bruno was the only dog still looking at her, suspicion lingering on his face.

"You shouldn't question your Beta, Fierce Pup," he muttered, and Storm blinked at him in stunned annoyance. Was he really going to lecture her about this? "Better be careful to gather the right plants—your recklessness could lead to dogs getting *more* sick, you know?" He turned away, not waiting for a reply, and followed Lucky toward the edge of the camp. Storm could only watch him go with her jaw hanging open.

What did I ever do to you? Storm wondered. A strange pulsing sensation was starting up between her eyes. *Most of the other dogs have accepted that Fierce Dogs aren't to blame for everything that goes wrong—why can't you?*

Storm grabbed another mouthful of grass between her jaws and tugged, her paws slipping slightly on the muddy bank of the river. The grass held firm for a moment longer, and then with a sucking, tearing sound it ripped free of its roots, spraying mud up into Storm's face.

Storm dropped the damp grass onto the growing pile by her side, blinked, and shook her head hard to try to throw off the mud droplets.

It's not a punishment. This isn't a punishment. I didn't do anything wrong. Lucky sent me because he trusts me. Because he knows I'll come back safely. It isn't a punishment.

It really felt like one, though.

Storm picked up her pile of wet, muddy grasses and trotted farther upstream, looking for a few more clumps to pick. Despite her annoyance at being sent to do this job, she wanted to do it well. She couldn't help thinking of poor Daisy and Thorn, wondering if she could have stopped them from getting sick in the first place. If only she had noticed the rotten prey earlier. Or if she had been brave enough to tell everyone the first time the prey had been tampered with . . .

She also didn't want to have to make two trips.

Storm sniffed and nuzzled through the grasses on the bank, looking for a bunch that she could get her jaws around, but as she walked she suddenly found her head had drooped and her eyes were almost closed. She wrenched her head up and made herself open her eyes. She couldn't sleep now. The sick dogs were relying on her.

There was no trace of foxes or coyotes, and for a moment Storm was almost disappointed. If she'd had to face down a bunch of sneering not-dogs, she would certainly be feeling more awake right now. . . . She bent to yank another bunch of grasses out of the muddy bank, and a sick, twisting feeling struck her, as if she might lose her balance and fall headfirst into the river. Pulling back, scrabbling on the slippery ground, she blinked and shook her head to clear the dancing lights that had formed in front of her eyes.

Panic gripped her. *I can't see!* She tried to focus on the scents around her, to ground her in the real world that felt like it was slipping away, but the flowing, changeable scents of the riverbank were too elusive.

Then there was something . . . something like a dog, but different . . .

Her head snapped up and she stared, wide-eyed, at the far bank of the river. A dog was standing there. The dancing lights had faded, and now everything was gray and strange, including the dog who turned his head to look at her, hackles rising, gray fur bristling.

Am I dreaming? First Blade, and now this . . . I'm sleepwalking, I must be!

She'd seen Blade in the shadows. She could believe that had been a trick of the light, but now . . . there was a familiar, impossible dog on the bank of the river, in broad daylight. Its form seemed to grow and shrink as Storm tried to pull it into focus, but she recognized the odd-colored eyes that somehow seemed to stay still even as the rest of the dog wavered and swam in front of her.

The half wolf had died on the frozen river too, a traitor who didn't deserve the name of Alpha, even though Storm had never known any other name for him.

"You're not there," she managed to huff. "You're dead."

Whether it was a ghost, a hallucination, or some trick of the Spirit-Dogs, her words seemed to stir the dog in front of her. It shook itself and vanished.

Storm walked to the river and slowly, carefully, dipped her

paws in, then her belly, and then finally plunged her head under the water. When she raised it again, the world seemed much clearer, almost as if she'd washed away fuzz that had grown over her vision.

I was wrong. This isn't a dream—but I'm not truly awake, either. I can't trust anything I'm seeing.

She knew she needed to sleep, but she didn't trust herself not to run off after visions of bad dogs. The thought of what would happen to any dog who got in her way, if she thought she was chasing Blade or the half wolf, made all her fur stand on end.

As soon as Daisy and Thorn are feeling better, and I've talked to Arrow about what we should tell Alpha, and I'm sure every dog is safe . . . then I'll go out into the forest and find somewhere to lie down.

Storm ran back to her pile of grass, shook herself hard to dry her fur a little, and then hurried back to camp, her heart pounding. All the way across the meadow and through the trees, she tried to keep her gaze focused on the hill up to the camp, and not pay too much attention to the strange shapes that she saw out of the corners of her eyes. She knew that they weren't real: The huge green beetles as big as her head were just leaves blowing in the morning breeze. The glinting yellow eyes of foxes in the undergrowth were only the Sun-Dog's light reflecting back at her, and the strange scent that filled her muzzle was the smell of the grass she carried in her jaws.

When she got to the Patrol Dogs' den, Daisy was inside, but Thorn was gone. Storm's heart skipped a beat, and she dropped the grasses quickly.

"Daisy, where's Thorn?"

The little white dog rolled over and greeted Storm with a soft whine. "Oh, please don't worry, Storm. She's feeling a little better. Moon and Beetle took her for a walk, to get some fresh air."

"Oh! That's good." Storm sagged with relief, although her heart didn't seem to want to slow down. It felt like it was beating high up in her throat. "Are you feeling any better?"

"A little," said Daisy, but her eyes were fixed on Storm. Storm felt suddenly as if she was standing in a ray of bright light. "What about you, Storm? Did you eat some of the bad prey too?"

Storm's ears flattened a little. "No. I'm fine."

"Well, maybe it's just me, but you look a little . . . off. Perhaps you'd better go back to your den too."

Storm hesitated, wrestling with herself.

I already decided I wouldn't lie down until I'd spoken to Arrow—until I knew what we were going to do to make this right.

But healthy dogs don't see things that aren't there. Maybe I am getting sick after all. Maybe a short rest, just a little one, would be good for me.

Storm looked around for Arrow as she came out of the patrol den, but she couldn't see him. That helped her make up her mind. She would just lie down—not in the den, where it was cool and dark and she might fall asleep, but at the mouth of the den, in the sunshine. She could watch the Pack and rest her bones until she was seeing things more clearly.

The camp was quiet, and very little moved in the clearing as Storm lay down and lowered her head onto her front paws. Most of the dogs seemed to be out on some errand or other, or maybe simply stretching their legs, keeping out of the way of the sick dogs. Storm saw Moon, Beetle, and Thorn returning to the patrol den, walking slowly, their tails flicking at one another. It was strange, she thought, how the two younger dogs were so much like their mother, both clearly Farm Dogs with their long fur and black-and-white coloring; and yet she could see Fiery in them both too. He was there in the extra few paws of height and breadth that they had, and in the way Thorn's ears folded down, rather than standing up like Moon's.

A commotion broke out near Alpha's den, and Storm's focus snapped to the source of the high-pitched yaps, her muscles bunching to leap up if she was needed.

But it was only the four pups coming out to play.

"Shush," said Alpha gently, following on their heels and settling down in a patch of sunlight. "Play quietly now, pups. There are dogs who need to sleep."

Nibble, Tumble, Fluff, and Tiny seemed to obey their Mother-Dog's words, rolling and playing on the grass in front of her with quiet enthusiasm. A warm feeling stirred in Storm's heart as she watched them. They were like little bundles of pure energy—it seemed impossible to keep track of them all at once.

Tumble seemed to be growing every minute. He was already up on his paws, running and bouncing all over the place. Nibble stalked a beetle—or maybe it was some invisible prey—in and out of her Mother-Dog's legs, while Fluff wandered from spot to spot sniffing at everything, as if every pebble and flower and twig were incredibly fascinating. Tiny struggled to run alongside her littermates, stopping every few steps to catch her breath, but Storm still couldn't keep track of her—she moved in fast bursts of energy, like a darting golden shadow. Somehow, despite her weakness, the little pup seemed to be everywhere at once.

And Wiggle . . .

Storm blinked, feeling as if a freezing wave from the Endless Lake had washed over her spine.

She could see him—her litter-brother, Wiggle, a dark shadow moving between the bright golden pups. He was playing too, chasing his tail or Tumble's, sniffing and stalking alongside Fluff and Nibble.

Storm knew that he wasn't there, that she was only seeing him because the sleeplessness was showing her visions of dogs who could not be real—but the more she watched him, the happier she felt.

We didn't get to play like this. We didn't get to enjoy the safety of our Mother-Dog's den, or live in a Pack that treasured us. Wiggle died so young—he never even got to choose his dog name. He never got to be part of a Pack at all.

Play, Wiggle. You deserve to have littermates for a while....

Storm tracked the shadow-pup's progress across the ground as best she could, watching as he scampered across the grass and then clambered over Alpha's legs . . . and suddenly her eyes met the swift-dog Alpha's, and Storm realized that Alpha was watching her, one ear cocked in a puzzled expression.

Storm looked away, her fur prickling with awkwardness. She closed her eyes, and when she opened them for another quick look, the shadow-pup was gone.

She let her eyes fall closed again and slumped down onto her side. If she was going to see nice visions like that, perhaps

195

imagining things wasn't so bad . . . but she knew that she couldn't pick and choose. If she wanted to see Wiggle again, she would also have to see Blade, and the half wolf, and imaginary foxes watching her from the trees. . . .

Storm shuddered, wishing she hadn't thought of foxes. She could almost hear them now, their strange not-dog words barely audible above the beating of her own heart. Or perhaps it was actually one and the same?

Waits. Watches. Waits. The moment comes.

Storm rolled over, suddenly jittery, as if she'd been asleep and a sudden noise had woken her. But she hadn't slept—she was still in the sunlit camp, could still hear the faint yipping of the four pups. She wriggled, twisted on her back with her paws in the air and her eyes shut tight, and then rolled again, but it was no good. Something was keeping her awake. She opened her eyes and her stomach dropped—she wanted to jump up and run far away, but she couldn't move.

Whisper's face was so close to hers she could have licked him on the nose. He wasn't wounded. He was lying beside her as if they were simply taking a quick nap together in the sunshine, his clumsy paws tucked up against his chest, his flank rising and falling gently. His short gray fur wasn't marked by a single scratch or drop of blood, and his eyes were alive again, not the terrible glazed dead eyes she had seen before.

Storm tried to pull away, but Whisper's gaze seemed to hold her fast.

"Storm, listen," he said. "You have to listen. . . ."

Storm woke with a yelp, her legs flailing as she rolled onto her paws and scrambled away from the spot where Whisper had been lying.

The camp wasn't drenched in sunlight now—it was still daytime, but the Sun-Dog had gone behind the trees and the light was softer and dimmer.

I was asleep, right in the middle of camp, Storm thought, half-hysterical. *I could have hurt some dog . . . I could have hurt the pups. . . .*

But there were no howls of pain or fear. She turned anxiously on the spot, but there didn't seem to be anything wrong at all. She could see Lucky and his hunting party standing near a new prey pile made of several large rabbits and a brown-feathered bird. Daisy was sitting outside the patrol den, looking much less shaky than she had before. It would be time to eat soon. Everything seemed to be fine.

So why did Whisper want me to listen? What did he want to tell me?

Storm shook herself hard. It wasn't really Whisper. It was just another imaginary dog, an invention of her exhausted mind, like Wiggle and Blade. Even now, she could see something moving in the shadows under the trees, and she made herself look away.

Enough. I've been seeing things all day, and I've had enough now. She sat down with her back firmly turned to the spot where she'd seen the movement. *I'm still so tired . . . whatever you are, just go away.*

There was a panicked growl from behind her, and a scuffling of paws against the ground. Storm flinched, half-convinced that it was still in her head, before she heard Bella's awful howl.

"I smell foxes!"

Storm spun around, nearly tripping over her own tail, just in time to see every member of the Pack rise to their paws with their hackles up. There was a rustling and a nasty, angry yowl, and then the scrawny red creatures burst from the undergrowth, sharp teeth snapping.

They were furious—and very, very *real*.

CHAPTER SIXTEEN

The foxes seemed to come from every direction at once. To Storm's shocked eyes they looked like they were swarming, like ants on a piece of rotten fruit. They snarled and snapped at the dogs, and several of them started tearing at the dens, digging out the bedding and breaking off pieces of the bushes that surrounded them.

"Pack, to me!" Lucky's bark rang out across the camp, startling the dogs into action. Storm stumbled over to him. "Stay together. Protect the camp. Protect Alpha!"

Oh no . . . The pups!

Two foxes were approaching Alpha's den, their skinny shoulders hunched. Alpha stood between them and the entrance, growling deep in her throat and showing her teeth.

Storm threw herself at the two foxes. She was still clumsy with exhaustion, but sheer momentum was on her side, and the foxes went sprawling under her. She got to her paws and stood flanking Alpha, making herself as Fierce-looking as she could and willing the foxes not to realize that she couldn't seem to focus on them properly.

"If you hurt my Pack," Alpha snarled behind Storm, "if your teeth graze so much as one hair on their coats, I will make you pay!"

"Bad dogs," the closest fox howled, fixing its yellow eyes on Alpha and the den mouth behind her. "Kills our cubs, drives us out. Foxes will have revenge!"

The creatures surged forward, their sharp teeth bared. Storm tried to get between the not-dogs and Alpha, knocking one back with a toss of her head that sent it flying. But the other fox swerved around her, its claws skittering on the earth, and Storm wasn't quick enough to stop it. She tried to catch it and drag it back, but her jaws closed on empty air.

"No!" Moon's howl of fear and anger rang in Storm's ears as the Farm Dog leaped and landed on the evasive fox's back, throwing it to the ground with one leg curled awkwardly under its body. The fox let out a whimper of pain, and a savage feeling of relief ran through Storm as she heard it. She stumbled back into her position flanking Alpha, wobbling on her paws.

Thank the Earth-Dog for Moon.

The camp was a blur of fangs and fur. The shapes of the foxes seemed to shudder in front of Storm's eyes, blurry streaks of red-brown, while the Pack Dogs were outlined with painful bright and dark shadows that trailed in the air behind them. Part of the patrol den was gone, torn away by foxes, but the dogs were fighting back: Through the trembling haze she saw Twitch's long hair and three legs, a blur of gold that could have been either Lucky or Bella, and a small tan-and-white ball of furious muscle that must be Snap.

Another fox lunged for Storm and almost caught her off-balance, but she made her legs stiff and refused to be knocked over. She let the fox hit her, and when its paws were tangled up in hers, she twisted her head to sink her teeth into the creature's neck. It gave a brief howl of pain before she shook it hard, one way and then another. The fox was as skinny as the others, but it felt suddenly heavy to Storm—she could barely drag it from side to side across the grass, and certainly couldn't shake it hard enough to snap its neck. The threat of it was enough to send the fox into a panic. It yapped and squirmed, and when Storm let go, it scrambled to its paws and fled the camp.

"Fox Coward!" shrieked another not-dog voice, and Storm turned to see a larger fox, the side of its face already bleeding, howling at the back of the creature she'd just driven away. "No dogs, no more!"

"Sunshine!" Alpha cried, the etiquette of rank forgotten in her panic. A fox had the Omega cornered and trembling. A vivid drop of blood ran down her shoulder, dark and sticky against the little dog's long white fur. Alpha bounded forward and raked her claws down the fox's pelt, opening deep wounds and dragging the creature back. It twitched and twisted to get away from the swift-dog's fury.

Storm felt sick with relief for Sunshine's safety, and sick with sadness at the memory of wounds just like those—the dog-claw wounds that had killed Whisper. She stared at the scrapping foxes and dogs and felt as if the ground had dropped out from beneath her paws.

This is happening because Whisper and a fox cub were both murdered. We drove the foxes out because of Whisper's death . . . but we were wrong. The dog who made this happen is here, right now, fighting alongside us.

Is that dog happy with what they've done?

The large fox that had howled after its retreating Packmate was staring at Storm, and she tried to pull herself together. Its eyes didn't quite meet hers—it was looking past Storm's shoulder, toward . . .

The pups!

Alpha had moved away from the den entrance to help Sunshine. Storm glanced behind her. Were those tiny golden ears she could see in the dimness beyond, and tiny glinting eyes peering out at the chaos?

For a moment, the large fox looked at the den mouth, and then at Storm. Everything went still, except that the not-dog creature itself seemed to pulsate, growing light and dark in time with Storm's thudding heartbeat.

Storm tried to leap for the fox, but somehow the fox had moved first. Her paws became huge and clumsy, and she fell, hitting the ground muzzle-first with a smack that rang through her head as if she'd been struck by a falling rock. She struggled onto her belly, but she couldn't get a grip on the ground to pull herself up, even when she heard the faint, high-pitched shriek of "Revenge!"

Even when another fox streaked past her toward the mouth of the den, even when the pups began to howl and cry . . .

A brown-furred dog landed heavily between the pups and the slavering jaws of the foxes. Her four paws hitting the ground sounded, to Storm, as loud and sudden as a roll of thunder.

Breeze!

"Back!" Breeze snarled, and lunged for the larger fox. "You

203

won't touch these pups!" She ducked and bobbed and sank her teeth into the fox's front leg and tugged, twisting her head so that the creature was pulled off its paws and thrown aside. It struck a tree trunk and lay dazed as Breeze turned to the second fox. It was smaller, and already backing away, but Breeze didn't hesitate—she charged, bowled the fox over, and bit fiercely into its throat. Blood bubbled up and ran into the grass.

Storm finally found the strength to get to her paws, and she staggered over to the mouth of the den and stuck her head inside. All four pups were there, pressed up against the thick branches at the back of the den, clinging to one another in a trembling bundle of gold and brown fuzz. The den stank of terror and of blood—Storm's vision swam with panic again, until she found the source of the smell. Four pairs of liquid eyes stared up at Storm, so wide they seemed like black pebbles in the pups' faces. Tumble was lying awkwardly between his litter-sisters, one leg wet with blood. He was whimpering, but awake.

"It's going to be all right," Storm said, and pulled back out of the den in time to see Breeze let the fox up, blood still streaming from its neck as it turned tail and streaked out of camp.

All at once, as if the wounded fox had given a signal, its Packmates stopped fighting and tried to retreat. Some of them vanished into the undergrowth as suddenly as they had appeared. Others had to dart and weave past the dogs' snapping jaws.

"After them!" Lucky howled. "We won't let them get away with this!"

Moon, Bella, and Alpha were the quickest to respond. They twisted and sprang after the foxes, barking insults and threats. A few more followed them, but the rest of the dogs simply stumbled back and lay panting on the grass, scratched and bruised.

Alpha skidded to Storm's side, kicking up a shower of dirt. She looked into the den, and her whole body seemed to sag. "Oh, thank the Earth-Dog and all the Wind-Dogs . . . oh, my poor pup, let me look at that leg. . . ."

Storm let herself sink down onto her belly, tiredness hitting her like a sudden rockfall. She stared at the camp, a cold shiver of dismay creeping over the back of her neck. The hunt and Patrol Dog dens were both torn apart, moss and leaves and twigs strewn across the camp, splintered branches hanging loose and twisting.

"Oh no," Twitch barked suddenly. "The prey pile! It's gone."

"Those . . . those . . ." Snap limped across the clearing to the place where the prey pile should have been, apparently unable to find a word bad enough for the foxes. "They took it all."

"Is any dog badly hurt?" Mickey yapped, and Storm held her

breath. There was a chorus of disgruntled whining and barking, but no dog cried for help.

"Come on, you have to come out so I can help you . . ." Alpha said gently, her head still inside the den, and a moment later there was a yelp of pain and she emerged with Tumble held carefully by his scruff. She laid him on the ground outside the den, and he gave another tiny howl as his wounded leg rested on the grass.

Lucky was at their side at once, staring down in horror at the blood that still oozed from what Storm could see now were tooth marks in Tumble's hind leg.

"It's a bad bite," Alpha said, between licks, keeping her tone light as Tumble looked at her with his tiny ears drooping. "You won't be able to run around for a little while, but we'll take care of you, and you'll be just fine. He'll be all right," she repeated, looking at Lucky. Lucky nodded.

"The others—?" he whined.

"They're fine," Alpha reassured him. "Thanks to Breeze!"

Alpha lay down with Tumble held closely between her front paws and began to wash him, and Lucky turned to Breeze with his ears flat against his skull. Breeze's muzzle was still stained with the fox's blood, but when she saw her Beta's expression of fear and gratitude, she dipped her head meekly.

"Breeze!" Lucky said. "I don't know how to thank you enough."

The other dogs gathered around, each of them barking their thanks to Breeze, and Breeze was quiet for a while, accepting their praise with a pleased expression.

"I didn't do anything special," she said. "No dog in the Pack would have let those horrible foxes harm the precious pups. I'm only sorry I wasn't quicker." She glanced down at Tumble, who quieted his whining and blinked up at her in wonder.

No dog in the Pack would have let them harm the pups. . . .

But I almost did.

Storm got unsteadily to her feet and padded over to Alpha. She stared down at Tumble's wound—as Alpha cleaned it, she could see the shape of the tear in his skin, the little chunk of golden fluff that was flapping loose. . . .

She looked away, feeling dizzy with shame.

"Alpha, I'm sorry," she whined under her breath, hoping the others would be too busy congratulating Breeze to hear her. "I was closest to the den. I should have protected the pups. . . ."

"Storm, you can't be everywhere at once," Alpha said impatiently, in between licks. "I know that you tried. Fortunately Breeze was here."

Storm backed off, feeling uneasy. Alpha was right; no dog

could fight off a Pack of foxes alone, and she didn't mean to suggest that she could, but . . .

I should have done better. If it hadn't been for Breeze, Tumble could have died, and it would have been my fault, no matter what Alpha says.

"We'll need to send out another hunting party," Twitch was saying. "And do something about the dens. We can gather new bedding, and perhaps some of these branches can be propped up. Come on, all unwounded dogs, to me—the sooner we make a start, the sooner we can eat and rest."

Storm completely agreed, it all had to be done, and they should do it soon . . . but she just couldn't.

I'm so tired. I'm not wounded, but I'm just so tired. I need to sit down, just for a little while, and then I'll help. . . .

She staggered to the edge of the camp, away from the bustle of activity that Twitch was building up. Her eyes were closed before she even lay down.

Just let me rest for a moment, and then . . .

A volley of loud barking woke her with a dizzying start, and she raised her head to stare blearily down the slope toward the pond. Colored blurs moved across the grass—one was dark, one white, one golden, and the last one was a struggling ball of fiery red.

"Look what we caught," Bella's voice called out, and Storm's bleary vision shuddered and pulled into focus three dogs: Moon, Bella, and Arrow, coming up the hill, triumph and anger in their faces. In Arrow's jaws, a small fox writhed and yelped, held tight by the scruff.

Dread and exhaustion mingled in Storm's heart as her eyes slid closed once more, and darkness closed over the camp.

CHAPTER SEVENTEEN

"Are you sick?"

Storm woke slowly, as if surfacing from beneath the lapping waves of the Endless Lake. Some dog was speaking to her, but she couldn't understand what he was saying. She wasn't sick. In fact, she felt much better than she had in days. When she opened her eyes, the world seemed clear and bright. More important, it seemed *real*. She wasn't sure how long she had slept, but it seemed to be early morning, and she was still curled up in the same spot on the grass as she had been when she'd gone to sleep.

There was a distinct, pleasant absence of pain. She hadn't realized that her heart had been beating irregularly, or that there had been a burning sensation in the back of her throat, until now, once those feelings had gone.

"Storm! Is there something wrong with you?"

All sorts of things, possibly. Or nothing. I can't be sure.

The thought finally prodded her into proper consciousness, and she sat up and stretched out, and then looked around to find Lucky sitting beside her.

"I'm fine," she said instinctively, feeling pleased that at the moment she actually felt that it was true.

"We need to talk," Lucky said. He sounded serious. Storm's ears pricked up, and she looked at him curiously.

"Is something wrong?"

"That's what I want to know. You've been fast asleep since the fight—you slept through sharing prey, even though Bella came and tried to wake you. Did something happen? Are you hurt?"

"I was just tired." Storm tried to reassure him. "I hadn't slept . . . last night. Before the foxes came," she finished, stumbling over the half-truth. She felt a prickle of anxiety as she looked into Lucky's eyes. There was concern there, but it was cold, somehow— his tail swished behind him in frustration.

"Why didn't you sleep?" Lucky demanded.

Storm hesitated, thrown by the directness of his question.

"I—I just . . ." she tried, but the words stuck in her throat. *I can't tell him why I kept myself awake so long. He might just tell me I'm imagining things, that I couldn't hurt any dog in my sleep . . . or maybe he'll tell me he agrees, and that I'm too dangerous to keep in the Pack. . . .*

"Storm, I'm just really disappointed," Lucky said. "Whatever your reasons for staying up all night, it was a foolish thing to do—a *puppyish* thing! You need to act like a grown dog if you want the Pack to treat you like one."

Storm bowed her head. At first, his words rolled off her back— she knew she had good reasons, and they were about as far from *puppyish* as she could imagine. *I'm doing this for you—for all of you!*

But the more Lucky went on, the more his telling-off started to sting. "You were slow and sleepy in the fight, and that put all of us in danger," he said. "It put the pups in danger!"

Just then, there was a pained whine from the direction of Alpha's den. Storm looked over and saw that Alpha and Moon were sitting with Tumble, who kept trying to walk on his bad leg and letting out little yelps. Moon fussed over him, telling him to stay still, but he kept straining to reach the spot of sunlight where his litter-sisters were playing, and then looking up at Alpha with sad, questioning eyes.

Storm's heart twisted with guilt. "I'm so sorry, Lu—"

Lucky cut her off. "I think you mean *Beta*."

Storm stopped, staring at Lucky. *It was a slip,* she thought. *I didn't do it on purpose! Why can't you give me even a little bit of a break?*

"Of course, Beta. I'm sorry," she said.

She certainly wasn't going to try explaining herself to Lucky when he was in this mood.

Tumble whimpered again, and Lucky's ears flattened for a minute.

"Good," he said. "Don't forget it again."

Storm looked around the camp, partly so that she didn't have to meet Lucky's eyes. It was amazing how much of the foxes' damage the dogs had fixed while she was asleep. Branches had been pulled and twisted around so that the hunters' den wasn't open to the sky anymore. The patrol den was almost completely destroyed, and it didn't look like they had tried to fix it—instead, the dogs had hollowed out another space beneath a different bush, biting off twigs and branches and moving rocks.

She felt another tremor of guilt in her paws at the fact that she hadn't helped them. The debris from the new patrol den seemed to be piled up in one corner of the clearing, at the foot of one of the large tree trunks, and she wondered if she could volunteer to help move it away later.

"Good morning, Beta," said a voice, and Storm looked around to see Rake and Ruff coming up the slope.

"Report, Rake? What did you see on the night patrol?"

"There's no sign of the foxes," Rake said. "Either they've run far away, or they're very well hidden, but we didn't scent them nearby."

Lucky frowned at the Patrol Dogs. "I don't like this. But at least we have our prisoner."

The prisoner! Storm couldn't believe she had almost forgotten—the last thing she'd seen had been Arrow returning with a wriggling fox held in his jaws.

She glanced back at the corner of the camp she'd thought was simply a pile of broken wood and rocks, and realized that the debris was very carefully positioned between the roots of a tree. There was a small gap between the pile of wood and stone and the tree trunk, just large enough to hold a small fox. Bruno, Mickey, and Bella were sitting around it, ears pricked and alert. *Guarding* it.

The sight reminded Storm again of just how much activity she'd slept through. She told herself she didn't care if Lucky thought she was being puppyish—she just wanted to do *something* to help out the Pack.

"What can I do, Beta?" she asked. "I could join a hunting party, or swap with one of the guards if you wanted. . . ."

"There's a hunting party out already," Lucky said. He was about to go on, when Tumble gave a yip of frustration. Lucky's expression froze. Then he met Storm's expectant eyes and bristled slightly. "They went out while you were asleep," he added, with a trace of spite that had Storm biting her tongue to stop herself from snapping at him.

I know you're worried about your pup, but I didn't bring those foxes here....

"In any case, I have a different job for you," Lucky said. He turned and barked across the camp, "Sunshine, are you ready?"

He enjoyed that a little too much, Storm thought gloomily, as she stuck her muzzle into a springy patch of moss, trying to sniff and poke just like Sunshine had showed her, to make sure she was picking only the best bedding material.

It was Omega work, tedious and arduous at the same time, and she didn't know how Sunshine could be so *happy* about it. The little white dog was snuffling through the undergrowth nearby, occasionally popping up with a mouthful of moss or soft leaves and dropping them into a pile.

"I'm so glad you're helping me, Storm," she'd said. "You've got such big, strong jaws, you can carry much more than me, so we'll only have to make a couple of trips! Isn't Beta clever?"

He certainly is.

Storm picked at the moss without much enthusiasm. She

supposed this would be good enough. She had tried to listen to Sunshine's instructions—despite her lowly rank, it was hard not to get swept up in her enthusiasm for even very, very boring things. But Sunshine talked so *fast*, and it had actually been quite complicated. . . .

Lucky is very clever. He knows just how to punish me without making it look like I'm being officially punished.

It would be fair enough—if I had done anything wrong.

Yes, she was pretty sure this patch of moss would be good enough. She leaned in and took a big mouthful in her jaws, ready to rip it up from the earth. . . .

"Yeowch!" Storm leaped back as a sharp pain stabbed into the top of her mouth.

"What's wrong?" Sunshine gasped, jumping out from behind a tree, her voice muffled by a huge mouthful of moss.

"Something sharp . . ." Storm dropped the moss and stared at it, dejected. Couldn't she even do a simple Omega task properly? "I thought I'd checked it!"

"Are you all right?" Sunshine said. "Open up."

Storm obediently opened her jaws wide and let the little dog peer inside.

"Oh, that must have hurt—it's just a tiny scratch, though.

You'll be fine." Sunshine turned to the hunk of moss and delicately picked through it. "Ah, do you see your problem? Look, here it is."

Storm looked, but for a moment she still couldn't see what had bitten her. Then Sunshine pulled the moss apart more, and she saw it—a twig with a sharp thorn growing through the middle of the soft, spongy plant.

"Let me show you how to check for thorns again," Sunshine began. "Though it'll be a bit harder with your great big paws . . ."

"I think maybe you should do the looking and I should just do the carrying," Storm said quickly. "No offense, Sunshine, but I really hope I don't need to learn too much about how to be a good Omega."

"Oh, none taken!" Sunshine said cheerfully. "Omega work's not for every dog."

Storm started collecting up the piles of moss, her heart warmed despite herself—only Sunshine could make the lowest, most unappreciated rank in the Pack sound like a job that only really *clever* dogs were suited for.

If only we could all find our places like she has, maybe we wouldn't fight so much. . . .

* * *

When Storm returned to camp with their last pile of bedding clutched in her jaws, the Sun-Dog was at his highest point overhead, and she was actually starting to feel a little too warm. New Leaf had been very welcome after the bitter chill and white storms of Ice Wind, but this was something different—it made her want to run down to the beach and splash in the Endless Lake. Perhaps she could, when she and Sunshine had finished putting the new bedding down. . . .

"Storm, there you are," said Lucky's voice from behind her. Storm tried to make sure that her cringing annoyance didn't show on her face when she turned to him.

"Yes, Beta?" she said.

"I have another job for you." Lucky came up to her, and she noticed that his ears were pricked up a bit more, and his tail held higher—he seemed to have lost some of the guarded anger from earlier, when he'd sent her off on her Omega errand. She wondered if Tumble was feeling better. "It's time for another dog to take over guarding our fox prisoner."

Storm felt herself stand up a little straighter. A flicker of hope stirred in her—this was an important job. Lucky wouldn't give this job to a dog he didn't think he could rely on.

"You need to stay *alert*," Lucky told her. "Listen for the fox trying to dig its way out. Don't let it distract you with talk. We must get this creature to tell us what the foxes' plans are."

"I'll be careful," Storm promised him, even though his words gave her an uneasy feeling. Just what *were* the foxes' plans—and what would the Pack do if those plans turned out not to be what Lucky was expecting?

The other two dogs on guard were Arrow and Woody.

"I'm glad you're here, Storm," Woody said, and Storm tried not to look surprised. "This . . . *creature* has been howling all morning, trying to get us to let it out."

"It's gone quiet now," Arrow added. He was looking thoughtful. "I wonder what it's thinking?"

"Perhaps it just knows that we aren't going to believe any of its foul not-dog lies." Woody sniffed. "We'll make an example of this fox, so the others will think twice before attacking our Pack again." He raised his head in determination. "We will finally get justice for Whisper."

Storm let her gaze stray to Arrow and found him looking back at her.

What can we say? We're sure the foxes didn't kill him, but no Pack Dog wants to hear it. This attack has just given them an excuse to go back to thinking the foxes are responsible after all.

"We'll see," Arrow said. "When Alpha questions this fox, perhaps we'll find out what really happened."

Storm nodded, hoping that at least Alpha would have the sense to listen to what the fox said and not dismiss it all as not-dog lies. She wondered suddenly whether Arrow felt any regret for catching the fox. She wanted to get to the truth as much as any dog, but if Woody was speaking for the majority of the Pack . . .

She tried not to think about it. There was no point until they'd heard what the fox had to say. Instead she focused on doing what Lucky had told her—scenting and listening carefully, her ears pricked for any sound of scraping earth or branches and rocks moving. If the fox escaped while she was on watch, she was sure Lucky would never ever let her forget it.

There wasn't any scrabbling from the fox inside the cage, but if Storm concentrated hard enough, she could hear its breathing and its paws padding on the earth as it paced around and around in the tiny space.

In fact, as Storm concentrated even harder and focused in on the sounds from the cage, she could hear something else too—a high-pitched muttering, almost too quiet to make out. The fox was murmuring something to itself.

"Not stay here," it was saying. "Nasty dogs, bad dogs. We go.

We get out. Home to Fox Father. We get home, cubs. . . ."

Horror shot through Storm, and all her fur seemed to stand on end. She glanced at Arrow and Woody, but neither of them seemed to have heard—or if they had, they hadn't understood.

This fox is pregnant!

The foxes believed—wrongly—that the dogs had killed a cub of theirs before. Now the dogs were in danger of doing just that. If they hurt this fox, or even killed her, her pups would die too.

Storm wondered, Would this change anything? Would the Pack find mercy . . . or would some dogs think that ending more fox lives would be *better*?

Storm shuddered and pawed the ground miserably. Perhaps the other dogs wouldn't think of that—just this once, she hoped it really was her Fierce, dark side giving her these thoughts, a darkness that the other dogs didn't have.

She had to believe that the Pack would do the right thing. The Pack wouldn't—*couldn't*—harm innocent pups . . . not even fox pups.

She wouldn't let them.

CHAPTER EIGHTEEN

Storm picked up her front paws one at a time, and then stood and leaned forward so that her spine stretched out, the stiff muscles in her neck and back creaking. As she sat up again, her stomach audibly rumbled. She'd missed last night's prey sharing and hadn't minded at first, but now the day was wearing on and she found herself drooling as she thought ahead to her next meal. The Sun-Dog was on the descent to his den beyond the Endless Lake, but it would still be a long time until he vanished completely.

In the cage of branches, the fox had stopped moving a little while ago, though its soft breathing and the occasional muttered curse on all dogs confirmed to Storm that it was still inside.

On the other side of the clearing, Storm saw Lucky and Alpha emerge from their den and dip their heads together for a moment. Then Lucky looked around the camp until he found Breeze, who was resting just outside the new patrol den.

"Breeze, can you come here a moment?" he barked. Breeze obediently stood, shook herself, and padded over to Lucky. "We'd like you to sit with the pups for a while," Lucky said.

"I'd be honored," said Breeze, her ears pricking up. "Can I ask, is Tumble . . . his leg . . ."

"He's doing well," Alpha said. She gave a small sigh, relief and tiredness mingling in her voice. "He's asleep now, and his leg is already healing. There may not even be any permanent damage— thanks to you."

Breeze looked incredibly pleased, and Storm hung her head a little as the brown dog sat down at the mouth of Alpha's den and peered inside.

No thanks to me.

She knew she had an opportunity to make it up to them, that she had been given an important job in guarding the fox, but there was a hollow feeling in her heart when she thought about that now.

She wanted to help the Pack. She wanted to do things that would make Alpha and Lucky trust her. But she couldn't let any dog hurt the pregnant fox. . . .

Lucky had fetched Twitch, and now the three lead dogs were

heading toward the cage. Storm sat up straighter, trying to ignore the twist of anxiety in her stomach.

Lucky, Twitch, and Alpha are all reasonable dogs. They're kind dogs. They won't do anything bad. They won't.

"It's time," said Alpha to Woody. "We need to interrogate the creature."

Behind them, the other dogs looked up, and one by one they got to their paws and followed, crowding around behind their leaders.

Woody seized one of the branches from the cage in his teeth. He braced his thick legs against the ground and pulled. For a second Storm worried that the whole thing would collapse, and the fox would be able to slip away through the trees and out of camp. . . .

Would that really be so bad?

She shook herself, trying to get rid of the traitorous thought.

The branch came away, leaving a hole easily large enough for a fox to run out through—but only if it wanted to run straight into the legs of Alpha, Lucky, and Twitch, and then all the rest of the Pack.

In a flash of puffed-up red fur, Storm saw the fox leap to her paws, turn on the spot, and then give a snarling hiss and back away, huddling against the trunk of the tree, as far from the dogs as she could get.

She looked very small. Her bushy tail was fluffed up and wrapped around to hide most of her body, which was only about as big as Sunshine's. Storm could see that behind her tail, her sides were slightly round. If she'd been a dog, she might have looked simply overfed, but her haunches and shoulders were as skinny as the rest of her kind—it was only the cubs inside her that had swelled her belly.

"Fox," Alpha said. "I am Sweet, Alpha of the Wild Pack. Do you know what that means?"

The fox did not reply. Her ears flattened to her skull, and her eyes were wide and dark.

"Your kind has attacked us for the last time," Alpha growled. "We will not let you go until we have the truth from you. Your pack attacked us once before in this place. You tore apart our home and stole our prey." She bared her teeth. "You tried to hurt our pups, but you were not successful. And worst of all, you attacked and killed an innocent dog on the borders of our camp."

Storm saw the fox's ears twitch, but she still hid her muzzle behind her tail and said nothing in reply to Alpha's list of crimes.

"If you don't answer, we will kill you!" Woody barked. "Then your pack will understand what it means to attack dogs in their own territory!"

A rumbling growl came from the fox, and she somehow pressed herself even tighter against the trunk of the tree, but she still said nothing. Storm's heart started to pound—if the fox refused to say a word, what could the others do? Would they simply follow through with Woody's rock-headed threat?

She wanted to give Lucky more credit than that, but she couldn't risk it. She had to do something.

"What is your name?" she said, trying to sound as stern as she could.

The fox stared at her, and still didn't answer, but its eyes narrowed just a little. Some of the fear went out of them.

"Why are you asking its name?" Woody muttered. "What does it matter? It's not a dog."

"My name is Storm," she went on, ignoring him. "This is Arrow. This is Lucky. That"— she glanced over her shoulder for the dog the fox could probably see most clearly—"that is Bella. What is your name?"

The fox let out a snort, ruffling the fur on its tail. "Dogs . . ." she muttered. She seemed to consider for a moment, and then raised her head just enough that her muzzle was visible. "Fox Mist is I. Stupids. What names? What is 'Bella'?" She gave Storm a thoughtful look. "You. At least you has a *true* name."

Alpha growled low in her chest, and Fox Mist shrank back once again. "Fox Mist, then. You have attacked our Pack, hurt our pups, and killed one of our dogs. What do you say to that?"

"Dogs kill!" Fox Mist howled, and Storm saw several dogs jump. "Dogs kill cubs, attacks foxes! No reason, but for *vicious*!" She sat up clumsily, flicking her tail out of the way and facing Alpha with what looked like the fox version of indignant pride. "*Dogs* attack. *Dogs* steal. Dogs takes everything. Takes and takes and takes," the fox spat. "No dens, no prey. What do foxes do? They takes *back*."

"And what about Whisper?" Twitch growled. "What did we do to you that meant you had to lure an innocent dog out of camp and kill him?"

Storm held her breath. The fox's gaze flicked from Twitch to Alpha to Storm.

"What dogs? What kill?" she said, low and uncertain.

"You know what dog!" Woody barked. "His name was *Whisper*, he was gray and short-furred, and he was a *good dog*. And you evil not-dogs killed him in the woods, in the middle of the night, and left his body for us to find!"

The fox glared at him. "Knows not," she snarled. "Foxes knows not evil. Knows only *survive*. Dogs comes to fox place, kills Cub Fire at dog place. Now dog dies at dog place . . . dogs say foxes kill?" Fox Mist shook her head. "Foxes not. *Dogs begin*. Foxes only finish."

Storm shuddered as a shocked murmur passed through the crowd of dogs.

"What is it saying?" Rake growled.

Storm knew exactly what Fox Mist was saying. She had come directly to the same conclusion that Storm had. If only the Pack would listen—but they were snarling and baring their teeth, raking their claws over the ground, angry and disbelieving.

"We should kill it," barked Ruff. "We must have revenge for Whisper!"

Dart and Woody howled their agreement, and several of the others gave uneasy, uncertain whimpers. Storm saw Bella and Arrow glance at each other, their ears pinned back. They seemed to be having another of their strange, silent conversations, before Bella stepped forward and spoke up in a loud, firm bark.

"We can't," she said. "She's our prisoner. That would be murder." Storm blinked gratefully at her, and then stared at Lucky.

You know the foxes didn't kill Whisper, she thought, staring hard, as if she could send her thoughts directly to his mind. *You don't want to believe it, but you know it's true. I told you, all of you. You can't let them hurt her. . . .*

Lucky hesitated, staring at something only he seemed to be able to see, and despite herself Storm gave an anxious whine.

"Woody, Ruff," said Twitch, turning to address his old Pack, "I know that you miss Whisper. I do too. But we're not Fierce Dogs—we can't kill a creature who is under our protection."

Storm hung her head. He was sort of right—Blade would not have hesitated to kill an enemy they had captive, not unless she had an even crueler use for them. Still, the words hurt, and the uneasy glances that Ruff and Woody were giving her hurt even more.

"Fox Mist does nothing to dogs," the fox snarled, and Storm could hear that she wanted to sound brave, but her voice was shaking. "Only breaks twigs, only to hurt dogs home as dogs hurt fox home! Dogs let Fox Mist go . . . foxes leave, no more attacks."

"Enough." Alpha was staring at her paws, but now she raised her head and fixed Fox Mist with a cold stare. "Our Third Dog is right: We are an honorable Pack; we do not kill for vengeance. But Woody is right, too: We must make sure that your kind leave us alone. Our Pack must be safe. We *will* make an example of you."

Fox Mist scrabbled back again, panic in her eyes, and Storm couldn't keep quiet anymore. She pushed herself forward.

"Alpha, wait. We can't hurt this fox. I heard her talking—and you can see for yourself—she's going to have pups. We can't hurt her if it risks harming them!" Storm watched Alpha, expecting her eyes to soften, thinking that she *must* change her mind.

Any dog who has been a mother would agree with me, right?

But instead Alpha's eyes narrowed. She glared at Storm, colder and angrier than ever.

"Why should that make a difference to us? These foxes attacked *my* pups, Storm. They wounded Tumble, and they would have done much worse if Breeze hadn't stopped them. And don't forget that foxes back in our old territory killed Moon's pup, Beetle and Thorn's litter-brother!"

Storm couldn't help casting an awkward glance at the three Farm Dogs. They looked away, hanging their heads with grief. Storm didn't want to upset them, but . . .

But that's all the more reason for us not to commit the same crime!

"Beta, please," she began.

Lucky bared his teeth at her, and then at Fox Mist. "We have to protect the Pack. Especially those dogs who can't protect themselves. . . ."

"No, wait," said a soft voice suddenly. Storm looked up, hope flaring in her heart, to see Moon stepping forward and meeting Lucky's and Alpha's gazes evenly. "Alpha, Storm is right. It wasn't *these* foxes that killed Nose. I miss him every day . . . but we don't have any proof that these foxes killed Whisper, just like they don't have any proof we killed their pup. If we kill this fox and her pups now, her pack will only attack us again and try to hurt our pups in revenge. It will never end!"

The silence that followed seemed to go on for a very long time. Moon and Alpha looked at each other, while the rest of the Pack seemed to hold its breath. Moon's ears twitched, and Alpha *huffed* through her nose.

Then Alpha gave a jerk of her head. "I will follow Moon's advice on this," she said stiffly. "We won't kill the fox, or its pups. It will be released back to its kind. But it deserves punishment," Alpha added. "We must devise some way to show the foxes that more attacks will not be tolerated."

There was another pause as each dog seemed to consider this—Storm was certainly racking her brain for some punishment she could suggest that wouldn't hurt the fox or risk her cubs, something that would make the Pack feel better without bringing the foxes back for yet more revenge. . . .

A movement caught her eye. Lucky had suddenly tilted his head, as if struck by a thought. He looked up at Alpha and spoke slowly.

"Alpha, do you remember when the Leashed Dogs first joined this Pack . . . when the half wolf believed I was a traitor? He wanted to give me a permanent mark, so that I would never forget it, and every dog would know."

Storm frowned. She didn't remember this—was it before Lucky and Mickey had brought her and her litter-brothers out of the Dog-Garden?

And why was Lucky bringing up anything the half wolf had tried to do? Surely they should be trying to do the opposite of what he would have done!

"We should mark this fox," Lucky went on, raising his voice, presenting his idea to the Pack. "Scar it, like Tumble will be scarred, so that the foxes will always remember what they did and know that if they attack us again, they will suffer the same."

Fox Mist hissed. "Does nothing to dogs," she muttered, panic rising in her voice. "Nothing! Dogs hurts foxes, for nothing!"

"It's kinder than what your pack tried to do to us," Alpha snarled. "Be quiet and hold still, and we will not hurt you as much. . . ."

"No, please, Alpha . . ." Storm blurted out. "This is wrong, it's savage!"

Alpha drew back and fixed Storm with a furious glare that made her paws tremble.

"*You* will scar the fox," she growled.

Storm wanted to say no, but the words stuck in her throat.

"Mickey, go with Storm and the fox," Alpha said, turning to the Farm Dog. Mickey's ears twitched, but he stood up straight and attentive.

"Yes, Alpha."

"Take Arrow, too—and Bella. You'll take the fox back to where its Pack was seen last. Storm will wound its leg and leave it for the other foxes to find. Storm, Arrow, Bella—*Mickey* is the leader of this mission, and you will all do as he tells you, do you understand?"

Storm thought she understood perfectly. Mickey was the only one of them who Alpha truly trusted. The other three of them were expected to do this to prove their loyalty to the Pack.

By harming an innocent fox who was only attacking us out of desperation. By making sure that the foxes will never leave us alone.

How could that be the right thing to do?

* * *

The journey was long, and it was miserable. The warmth that Storm had enjoyed earlier had abruptly slipped away as the Sun-Dog hid his face behind a thick bank of gray cloud. The dogs were forced to walk slowly, in tight formation around Fox Mist so that she couldn't get past them and escape. They didn't talk, and they couldn't run, so there was no sound but the stirring of the wind in the trees and the dogs' own breathing, interrupted every so often by a soft whimper of fear or exhaustion from the fox.

Storm was bringing up the rear, walking so close to Fox Mist that she had to keep watching where she put her paws, in danger of treading on the fox's tail. She felt sick with herself, and sick with the whole Pack for their rock-headedness.

Why did I speak up? It's only a wound. I've wounded before—foxes, dogs, coyotes, not to mention prey creatures.

But that had been in the heat of battle, or during a hunt. This was different—it was so *cold.*

Fox Mist stumbled, and Storm nearly walked over her. The huddle of dogs came to a halt, and Mickey twisted back to look at the fox, dipping his head to be nearer level with hers.

"Come along," he said, without much feeling, but without any cruelty either. "It isn't far now. I can scent the foxes ahead."

Fox Mist made another whimpering sound, took a step

forward, and then as quick as Lightning running across the sky she turned and threw herself between Arrow's paws, slipping under his belly—but Bella was too quick for her, seizing her scruff and dragging her back like a naughty pup.

"Too slow," she said, her voice muffled through a mouthful of thick red fur. She wrangled the fox back into place, and Arrow closed up the gap again.

They walked on, trudging over the grass, with Mickey sniffing for any sign of the foxes and Storm bringing up the rear, her steps growing slower and slower. With every plodding pawstep, her heart felt heavier, until she thought she couldn't carry it any farther.

"I think this is far enough," said Mickey, in a low voice, raising his nose to scent the air. "The foxes are close. If we do it here, they'll find her soon and she'll be all right."

Storm couldn't. She already knew it, deep in her stomach.

She looked at Mickey, the dog who had found her in the Dog-Garden with Lucky, who'd helped her escape the coyotes, who'd always been kind and fair. He didn't want this, she was sure, or he wouldn't care whether the fox would be all right. . . .

Then she looked at Bella—she was so cunning, so willing to bend rules and keep secrets if she thought it was the right thing to do. And Arrow had given up everything he ever knew, his loyalty to his family and to Blade, to join Sweet's Pack and warn them that they'd been betrayed.

Alpha had sent them all to prove themselves, but perhaps that had been foolish of her. Perhaps Storm could still do the right thing.

"Bella," she said, "Arrow . . . We can't do this."

"Storm, come on," Mickey began. "It's Alpha's orders."

"But we know the truth! We know the foxes didn't kill Whisper, and we all know that if we do this, they will only retaliate again. It's like we're chasing our tails 'round and 'round, and all that happens is we bite ourselves. This isn't getting us any closer to justice!"

Fox Mist glanced up at Storm, a terrible hope growing in her eyes.

Don't look at me like that, Storm thought. *I haven't convinced them yet. . . .*

Arrow and Bella glanced at each other, and then looked away, their tails between their legs.

"You're right," Arrow said. "But we've been sent on this mission for a reason, Storm. If we don't follow Alpha's orders, she will never truly trust us." He looked up at Storm, and his pointed ears twitched. "You know that we need all the allies we can get."

He means me and him, Storm thought. *The Fierce Dogs.*

"You weren't part of our Pack when I allied with the foxes," Bella said. Between them, Fox Mist's ears turned to Bella in surprise.

"I heard about it . . ." Storm began.

"It took me a long time to regain the Pack's confidence. I agree that hurting this fox will do no good . . . but if it's Alpha's order, we should follow it."

"But it's only the four of us here, and we were already supposed to let her go," Storm said. "No dog needs to know we didn't wound her. Mickey . . ." She looked up at the Farm Dog's kind face. "You heard Bella and Arrow—they *know* this is wrong, they're just too scared to do the right thing."

"Hey!" Bella complained, but Storm kept her eyes fixed on Mickey.

"I don't know. If we don't show the foxes that we're in charge here . . ." Mickey began.

"Dogs," said Fox Mist suddenly. "Dog Storm. Dog . . . Mi-ckey. Fox Mist promises, dogs lets us go, leaves us whole, foxes goes.

Goes far away, keeps peace, never returns."

"How can we believe that?" Mickey said, but there was hesitation in his voice.

"You'll tell them that we were merciful," Storm said, lowering her muzzle to speak directly to the fox. "Won't you? You'll tell them that we could have hurt you, or even killed you, but we didn't want to harm an innocent fox or her cubs. We didn't kill that cub, and we don't all believe you killed our friend—we just want peace."

"Yes. I tells." Fox Mist swished her bushy tail enthusiastically. "Tells foxes. Keeps peace. All foxes wants."

Expectantly, Storm, Bella and Arrow turned their heads to look at Mickey.

"How can you want me to wound her now?" Storm whined.

Mickey closed his eyes for a moment. "I'm going to regret this, aren't I?" he muttered.

"I hope not," Storm told him.

Mickey's tail swished against the ground once, twice, and then he stepped back. "Go," he growled. Before his growl had even finished, Fox Mist had taken off, faster than a rabbit, her small body low to the ground. "And remember your promise!" Mickey barked after her, as she vanished into the undergrowth without looking back.

Storm felt her heart lift, as if it had been weighed down with rocks that she'd finally swept away.

Bella and Arrow were both looking at her, anxious expressions on their faces.

"I hope you know what you're doing," Bella muttered.

"The right thing," said Storm. "I'm sure of it."

CHAPTER NINETEEN

Lucky was waiting by the entrance to the camp when the four dogs returned. As they walked up the hill, the Sun-Dog running down the sky behind him made his fur glow golden but his face seem very dark.

"Report, Mickey," he said, as soon as they were close enough to hear him.

Mickey stayed quiet, his head down, until they reached the edge of the camp and he could sit beside Lucky and look him straight in the eyes. Storm's stomach twisted . . . had he changed his mind? Was he going to tell Lucky what she'd done?

"All went well," Mickey said. "Storm did her duty. We left the fox near their old camp—she'll be found soon, if she hasn't been already. We won't have any more trouble with the foxes."

Lucky tilted his head, trying to look into Storm's eyes. She met his gaze evenly, despite the thudding of her heart. . . .

But no, this is wrong, she thought, panic swirling around her head. *I wouldn't be feeling calm and meeting his eyes, not if I'd just had to wound that fox. Lucky knows that. He knows me. I should be angry, uncomfortable, breathing hard. . . .*

I'm never going to get away with this. . . .

But Lucky didn't seem to see anything strange about the way Storm looked—perhaps she'd made herself so nervous he mistook it for discomfort and anger. Either way, he blinked and dipped his head to Mickey.

"Well done, Mickey. And well done, the rest of you. It wasn't an easy task, but you've done something good for the Pack. Alpha will be proud."

You're right, Storm thought, *we have—just not the thing you think we've done.*

He would never trust her again, or any of the others, if he found out what had really happened. But Storm couldn't make herself regret it. She had spared another creature undeserved pain, and that felt *good*—as if she had shone a bright light into the dark places in her own heart.

"Excuse me," came a muffled voice from behind them. "Coming through." Storm turned and shuffled aside when she saw

Bruno, Snap, and Dart coming into camp with prey creatures dangling from their jaws. Bruno and Dart each had a rabbit, but they looked rather small, and Snap was only carrying a pair of skinny ferrets.

"Stupid foxes," Bruno muttered as he passed. "The prey pile was full before they came. . . ."

"We'd just filled it up," Mickey agreed. As Snap passed, he bent his head close to hers, and Storm heard him murmur, "Did something go wrong? There's so little!"

"Just bad luck," Snap replied, nudging the top of her head against the fluffy underside of Mickey's chin. "It'll be better tomorrow."

"Pack, to me!" barked Alpha. Snap trotted over to the prey pile and dropped her catch alongside Bruno's and Dart's meager offerings, and Storm followed, dragging her paws a little. "It's time to share prey," Alpha said, and then sighed as she looked down at the small pile. "Listen, every dog. We will eat in Pack rank, as usual. But before we do, I want you all to give some thought to the dogs who will come after you."

There was a pause, while all the dogs came to sit around the pile, looking at the rabbits and then at one another. Storm couldn't help glancing at Sunshine. There were plenty of dogs who ranked between Storm and the Omega, including all the

Patrol Dogs—Moon, Daisy, Thorn, and Beetle, even Breeze—but still, it was Sunshine who she hoped most strongly would be able to eat that night.

"Now, let's eat," Alpha announced, and stepped forward. She tore into the first rabbit delicately, ripping away a chunk of meat, and then stepping back. She chewed it slowly, though Storm was sure she could have swallowed it in one go if there was more to go around. Lucky took even less than his mate, and the rest of the dogs followed their example. When Storm's turn came, she almost wondered if she should refuse altogether.

Lucky and Alpha were both so angry with me . . . and what if they know what I did, and they're just not letting on?

But in the end, she did go to the prey pile and take a very small bite. It was only enough to sharpen her hunger, really, but she comforted herself with the knowledge that all the dogs would be feeling the same. Tomorrow—if Lucky would let her—she resolved that she would go out on a hunt, and she wouldn't return unless they could feed the Pack properly.

When all the hunters had eaten, Alpha stood up. "Patrol Dogs, wait a moment. There is something that needs to be said. Moon, will you come forward?"

The white-and-black Farm Dog glanced at her pups, then at

Twitch, and then stood up and walked toward Alpha.

"You fought very bravely against the foxes, Moon," Alpha said. "You defended your Pack nobly, and your valor hasn't gone unnoticed. Your punishment is ended. From now on, you will eat in your rightful place, at the head of the Patrol Dogs, and you will no longer be on High Watch."

Moon gave Alpha a low bow and dipped her ears gratefully. Beetle yapped with happiness, and a ripple of relief ran through the Pack, hunters and Patrol Dogs alike. Storm forgot her tension and her hunger, letting her tongue hang out with joy.

"There is one other thing," Alpha said. "Though Moon has been relieved from High Watch, I believe that these dangerous times call for it to become a permanent part of our patrol routine. Every dog will take turns, including some of the hunters when there are too few Patrol Dogs available. Tonight, it will be Storm's turn on High Watch."

So they are still angry with me, Storm thought, as she dipped her head in respectful agreement. *They could have chosen any dog, and they chose me.*

The high rock on the cliff above the camp was just as windy, and even colder than when Storm had visited Moon there. With the

Sun-Dog fast asleep in his den, the Endless Lake seemed to give off great waves of cold that washed up on the beach and crept up through the ground and into Storm's paws. She shivered and turned on the spot just like she'd seen Moon do.

If she was being punished, she would rather be *told* that she was, and what she had done—in front of the whole Pack, if necessary. Then at least she would know if she was still being punished for protecting the Pack by trying to stay awake, or for protecting the Pack by letting the fox go unharmed, or for some other crime she couldn't justify to herself so easily.

The clouds that had blocked the Sun-Dog had shredded into wispy pieces now, and the Moon-Dog almost seemed to be playing chase with them as they skimmed across the sky. She darted in and out of their shade, glinting on the choppy waves of the Endless Lake and then hiding away again. Storm wished she could be up among the stars playing chase with the Moon-Dog—she would be able to see even more than she could from High Watch, and at least she wouldn't have to be sitting still all night.

She stared down toward the camp, imagining the other dogs curling up in their new dens, sleeping on the moss that she and Sunshine had gathered, and then went very still and slowed her breath, trying to listen to the sounds of the camp and the land all around it. Her best shot at knowing if an attack was coming in the dark would be to hear it—although she wasn't expecting one, the thought of missing any sign of impending danger made her shudder.

The cold air and the rumbling in her belly kept Storm awake for a long while, but when the Moon-Dog had wandered a little way across the sky, she felt her eyelids start to droop. She got to her paws, shook herself hard from head to tail, and started to pace, trying to focus on the feeling of the rough, cold stone and sand.

Suddenly she heard pawsteps that were not her own. They were coming toward her, up the path—more than four paws, from the sound of it. . . .

She sniffed the air carefully, and then relaxed. The scents were familiar—Pack scents. Breeze and Thorn strode out of the darkness.

"Hello, Storm," said Thorn, bounding up the path, her long fur blowing in the cold wind from the Endless Lake. "We're on night patrol, so we thought we'd come past and see how you're doing."

"Anything to report?" Breeze asked.

"No, nothing," said Storm.

"Mother says, if you go a little farther down there's an

overhanging rock. If it rains, you can shelter under there and still have a good view of the camp." Thorn wagged her tail. "And you can roll on the sandy bits of the earth to warm up your back."

"Thanks." Storm blinked happily at Thorn. "Thank Moon for me too, won't you? I really appreciate it."

"No problem," Thorn panted.

"Storm, I have to ask, if you don't mind. . . ." Breeze padded up and sat near Storm, looking out over the glinting black surface of the Endless Lake, as if she was shy of meeting Storm's gaze. "It must have taken a lot of courage to follow Alpha's orders and scar that fox. We could all tell you didn't want to do it. What happened, when you got out there?"

Storm tried to breathe evenly. "I didn't want to, it's true. But we had to follow Alpha's orders. She was right—we had to punish the fox." She was shocked how easily the lies came.

"What was it like?" Breeze whispered. "Actually wounding the fox like that?"

Storm shuddered. "It . . . it was . . ." She fished into her memory for other wounds she'd made, but she knew that in the heat of a battle or a hunt wasn't the same.

"Oh, Storm. Was it so terrible? Did it . . . did it struggle?" There was horror in Breeze's voice.

"She wasn't happy," Storm said. "She . . . yes, she tried to get away . . . it was . . . bloody," she finished, feeling sick with herself, hoping that it would be enough to put Breeze off asking any more.

"Well, they should think twice about attacking the Pack again now," Breeze said, giving a brief shiver and then getting to her paws.

"I hope so," Thorn said quietly. "I hope it doesn't just make them angrier."

"Come on, Thorn," said Breeze firmly, as if determined to change the subject. "We'd better get on, or we won't be able to cover enough ground before dawn."

"All right—good night, Storm," Thorn said, dipping her head as they started back down the slope.

"Good night." Storm watched them go, waited for a moment longer, and then padded down in the direction Thorn had shown her. Sure enough, the rock jutted out and up, as thick and solid as a huge tree trunk, and underneath it was a space big enough for a dog to shelter where she could still see out over the camp, and over the lake in the other direction. It was a little warmer there, protected from the worst of the cold wind, and Storm huddled down gratefully, hoping that she would warm up soon.

Storm mostly listened and watched for movement near the camp—for foxes, or coyotes, or any sign of the bad dog who had caused all this trouble. But finally she did glance over at the dark lake, and she saw something strange. There were lights, out on the lake where she knew there was nothing but water. They were too bright and too low to be stars, and too small and too steady to be the reflection of the Moon-Dog. Unless the stars had fallen into the lake and were bobbing gently on the surface. She considered that possibility for a while, before she realized what she had seen floating on the lake before.

A longpaw floatcage!

It had to be. Only longpaws and Spirit Dogs could make light like that.

Storm stared at the lights, her hackles raised, ready to howl the alarm if necessary—but how would she know if it was necessary? Would it come closer, or would it just stay out there on the lake?

Storm had had only had a few brief encounters with longpaws, and they had all been frightening and strange. But she wondered if that had been because the longpaws were alone, cut off from the rest of their Pack. Longpaws used to be everywhere before the Big Growl—at least according to Lucky and Mickey. Lucky had lived in their city, hunting for their scraps instead of for prey, and Mickey had even lived in one of their houses! When he spoke about them, they didn't sound so bad—almost like being in a Pack where your Alpha was a longpaw and they made sure you had food and somewhere warm to sleep, but in return you had to give up your freedom.

Some dogs might like that, Storm thought. *Things would be much simpler.*

But Storm knew it wasn't a life for her. She would rather go hungry some nights, as long as she could run and play and defend her own territory, and not have to bow to some creature she couldn't even understand.

What would it be like if they came back? If there was a longpaw in every house in the lake town, and loudcages running up and down the streets all the time? Would they bother the dogs, scare away the prey? Would they try to make them come and live in their houses and wear collars like the Leashed Dogs had? What would they do if the dogs didn't want to go?

Perhaps they would never come back. The floatcage was bobbing farther away now, its lights dwindling until they were just a flickering dot on the dark horizon. Storm watched until they had vanished altogether.

I'll report it to Alpha in the morning, she thought. *There's nothing to be afraid of right now.*

The thought felt so comforting. She knew it wasn't true—there were still coyotes, and she didn't know for certain how the foxes would react to Fox Mist's return, and under it all there was the threat of the bad dog, and her own dreams. . . .

But here on High Watch, the world felt so peaceful and quiet that her eyelids started to get heavier again. She shivered.

Can't fall asleep. I'm on watch. I'll get up in a moment and walk again.

Any moment now . . .

Storm stretched out luxuriously, turning her belly to the sky and feeling the sweet warmth of the Sun-Dog soak into her coat. The earth beneath her was warm too, and she flicked an ear lazily to dislodge a small insect that had mistaken her for a blade of grass.

She was in the camp, and the Pack was with her, all around her—she couldn't see them, but she could hear them, snuffling and yawning, talking in low and gentle voices, simply existing. Their scents were familiar and comforting. She felt safe.

She wriggled her back against the warm ground and flopped onto her side. The gray dog beside her gave a happy huff, stretched out his paws toward her, and then drew them back into his chest, folding them like a pup. She leaned over and

251

gave him a quick, friendly lick on his nose.

"I'm so sorry you died," she told him. "But it wasn't my fault, was it? I'm not the one who hurt you."

It felt so obvious now, she wondered how she could ever have thought anything different.

Whisper gave a bark of laughter. "Of course not," he said, his brown eyes bright. "You never did anything but protect me. You're a Good Dog, Storm. I always knew it. You fight for us even when no other dog can. You even fought for the foxes."

Storm felt heat under her skin, prickling like embarrassment, but it was a pleasant feeling. She wanted him to go on, and she didn't feel guilty for wanting it either.

"I've spent so long thinking I must be Bad," she said.

"You are Fierce and Good," said Whisper, with an amused flick of his ear. "Whatever dog said you couldn't be both must have had rocks for brains. You were right to let the fox go." He shifted so that his body was closer to hers. She let him. It was funny—she never would have wanted to be so close to him while he was alive, but now she felt comforted by his warmth.

The day seemed to be growing colder. She glanced up, looking for the Sun-Dog, but she couldn't find him. Instead a dark shadow was falling over the sky . . . a shadow with a strong jaw, four paws, and two pointed ears.

The great Fierce Dog loomed over the Pack, pacing silently overhead, his *dark eyes scanning the landscape. They looked down on Storm for a moment, and she felt as if she was being pinned to the ground—as if those eyes could see into her heart, pick out every dark thought she had ever had, every embarrassing moment, every impulse and feeling. It knew when she had been happy, and when she had lied, and when she had done the best she could. . . .*

Then the great dog passed over the camp and walked on. The Sun-Dog stretched and woke, and the camp was flooded with light and warmth once more.

"Was that the Fear-Dog?" she asked, in a hushed voice, half-afraid that she would summon the dog back again. "Is the Fear-Dog really real?"

"I'm not sure," Whisper admitted. "Maybe he is. Something is stalking us. The darkness is here, Storm. It's in the Pack. We need a dog who can protect us all, like you do." He looked into her eyes. "I believe in you."

"But how can I . . . ?" Storm murmured, and blinked.

She was back on High Watch, and the dawn was breaking over the trees, sending bright rays of light into her sheltering spot under the rock overhang. The Sun-Dog warmed her, and she twitched onto her paws, feeling guilty for falling asleep . . . but at the same time, she felt comforted, and *confident*, in a deep place in her heart that had felt nothing but unease ever since Whisper's death.

"I did not do this," she said out loud, knowing nobody but

the Wind-Dogs would hear her. "Something is wrong in the Pack. There's a darkness here. But it's not in *me*, and that means I can find it and I can stop it."

Feeling as if she could do almost anything, Storm shook herself out and then started down the slope toward the camp.

CHAPTER TWENTY

Most of the dogs were just getting up when Storm arrived back in camp. They lay outside their dens or padded around one another, stretching and yawning. Storm saw Daisy mournfully sniffing at the place where the meager prey pile had been, and realized many of them must still have empty bellies from the night before. But although Storm hadn't had any more to eat than Daisy, she didn't feel the hunger now.

I can fix that too. Just let me get out there to hunt, and I'll bring us back a feast.

Well, she would do her best, anyway.

Storm couldn't help glancing up to the place in the sky where she had seen the great dark dog in her dream, but she couldn't see anything there but clouds and sky, and the occasional swooping lake bird.

She trotted over to Alpha's den, eager to give her report, and found Breeze and Thorn there already. Alpha was nowhere to be seen—perhaps she was still in the den with the pups. Thorn was speaking to Lucky and Twitch, casting occasional glances back to Breeze as if to have her confirm what she was saying.

"The only fox-scents we could find were old," Thorn said. "At least a day—so they haven't been back since the attack. There was nothing else."

"Thank you, Thorn, Beetle," said Lucky. "You may go, get some rest."

Twitch turned to Storm, and his long, floppy ears pricked up in greeting. "Hello, Storm," he said. "How was your first night on High Watch? Do you have anything to report?"

"Only that I saw something on the Endless Lake," Storm said. "It was another one of those longpaw floatcages. It was carrying bright lights, so I knew it must be a longpaw thing. It didn't come too close, though—it just bobbed about out there for a little while and then vanished."

Lucky frowned. "I'll tell Alpha later," he said. "I don't want to bother her now, while she's with the pups."

"Can I ask, Beta, how is Tumble doing?" said Storm. She was ready for him to snarl at her, but instead he gave a placid nod.

"He is recovering well," said Lucky. "He's feeling a lot better, and the fox bite is healing nicely. He will be able to walk again soon. And it's about time," he added, with a happy sort of whine. "We were up half the night trying to keep him down. That pup will be impossible to keep track of when he's older."

"I'm so glad," Storm said. *And not just for Tumble's sake. I'm glad that you're feeling better too.*

"You should get some sleep," Twitch told her. "You must be tired after standing guard over the fox yesterday and then going straight to High Watch."

Storm felt a little shudder of guilt—she wasn't half as sleepy as she should have been—but she didn't contradict him. "Thank you, Beta," she said to Lucky, and trotted over to the hunters' den. She picked a spot just outside it and turned a hasty sleep circle before settling down and pretending to nap. She kept her eyes just slightly open, watching the rest of the dogs.

There is darkness here . . . but I can't see it. There was no dog who didn't seem like they belonged, like they didn't love their Pack. What kind of dog could kill their Packmates, poison and manipulate them, but never give any impression that they were scheming?

And why would they do it in the first place?

Storm tried not to chase her thoughts off in all directions

like a puppy with a brace of rabbits, but instead focused on simply observing the Pack.

A little while later, she saw Lucky come into the middle of the camp and heard him bark, "Hunters, to me!"

She got to her paws at once, wide-awake and eager to get involved, and trotted over to Lucky's side.

"We need to put together a hunting party—we must ensure the Pack eats well tonight."

Bruno's stomach audibly rumbled as if in reply, and Mickey chuckled at him.

"Arrow, Bruno, Snap, and I will go," Lucky said. "And Breeze will be our scout dog."

"I'd like to come," Storm volunteered, her eagerness getting the better of her.

"I'm not sure," Lucky said, though he seemed more thoughtful than reluctant. "You're still young, and you've never had a night watch before. You need your rest. . . ."

"I've had a rest," Storm yapped. "I'm fine—I'd really like to help."

Lucky hesitated for a moment longer, then barked his approval. "All right, you can come—you'll be useful."

Storm felt she was almost glowing with pride. Perhaps

Lucky truly had forgiven her.

When they left the camp, Storm's mood was high. They would find plenty of prey, and the whole Pack would eat well. She would prove her usefulness to Lucky and Alpha, and Tumble would get better, and they would forgive her for her carelessness—and she would be able to put the whole incident with Fox Mist behind her, too.

However, only a few pawsteps into their hunt, Storm could tell something was wrong. The land seemed still, more so than usual. The sounds and scents of prey were faint and muffled, when she could pick them up at all. For a moment she wondered if there was something wrong with her—did she need more rest after all? Could she not trust her senses?

But then she saw the others looking confused, too. They sniffed at the ground and the air as they ran, as if they were feeling the same way Storm was. They reached the line of trees, where Storm would expect to at least be able to hear birds singing and pick up the stale scent-trails of badgers and other creatures who roamed the woods at night. But there was still nothing, and Lucky brought the party to a halt, his muzzle creasing in confusion.

"Where are the Wind-Dogs?" Snap whined, and Storm almost wagged her tail in relief. Of course, *that* was why the scents couldn't seem to reach her—there was no wind to carry them. The branches and leaves on the trees were hanging almost perfectly still, and the Sun-Dog's gaze felt hot and stifling on the back of her neck. It was as if all the wind had blown past her overnight, out of the Endless Lake and away, leaving the land here strangely warm and quiet.

"They'll be back," said Lucky. Storm knew he was right—the Wind-Dogs couldn't just *leave*, could they? "Let's press on."

"I'll circle more widely," said Breeze, "and see if I can find any scents."

"Good idea," said Lucky, and Breeze immediately picked up her paws and darted away. "Come on, let's go through the woods and head toward the river. We should be able to smell whether there have been rabbits in the meadow recently, even if we can't pick them up from far away. Keep scenting around—perhaps we will find something we aren't expecting."

Storm followed his instructions, keeping her muzzle high and sniffing all around as they passed through the woods, but even though she saw several birds shuffling along the branches high above, and at one point she thought she heard the scrabbling of a prey creature nearby, she still couldn't scent a single thing except the wood itself. The earth and the trees seemed to release a stronger scent than ever before, especially where the Sun-Dog's gaze hit them.

The dogs emerged into an open space, where they could see the glinting line of the river winding through the grass. Storm knew there were frequently rabbits here, or sometimes even fat, lazy pigeons who could be caught by a cunning and quiet dog. There might even be a river-rabbit down by the shore. But if they were nearby, she couldn't scent a single one. Lucky led them down to the river, and they trod carefully along the bank a little way, but there was no sign of any tasty river creatures either.

"Let's stop to drink," Lucky ordered after a little while. "It's so warm today, and when the Wind-Dogs return, we'll want to be ready."

The dogs all stopped gratefully and bent their heads to lap up a few mouthfuls of water from the clear river. Storm padded into the water, just so it came up over her paws, and then rolled so that her coat soaked up the cool water. She rolled to her paws, shook it off again, and immediately felt better.

There was a gentle thudding of pawsteps, and Breeze hurled into view behind them, crossing the meadow in what seemed like a few long strides.

"Nothing," Breeze gasped as she reached them. "I went so far, but I couldn't find a trace of a living creature anywhere."

"Perhaps they're all hiding from the Sun-Dog," said Bruno, panting. "He's very strong today."

"Could the Wind-Dogs be angry with us?" Arrow asked Lucky. "Is there anything we could do to tempt them back?"

Storm raked her paw across the wet pebbles uneasily. Surely that couldn't be it . . . they hadn't done anything to make the Wind-Dogs cross, had they?

Her ears twitched as a light breeze stirred the wet hair on the back of her neck.

As one, all six dogs looked around, their ears pricking up and their mouths opening to taste the faint scent that blew past them. It was coming from upstream, and as the breeze blew stronger, Storm started to recognize it—a light, tasty, spicy scent of a living creature. A prey creature . . . but one that carried a strange edge to its scent. It was unique. It was . . .

Lucky gasped, his tongue hanging from his jaws in delight. "I smell the Golden Deer!"

The Wind-Dogs are teasing us.

Storm imagined that the invisible Spirit Dogs must be enjoying themselves immensely, like puppies playing with a beetle or a mouse, watching from above as the hunting party sprinted upriver, paused, lost the scent, found it again, followed it inland, chased it through a stand of tall white trees and over a hill and around a pile of rocks, then lost the scent again. . . .

Each time Storm caught that strange and wonderful scent, she felt energized, as if she could run and run forever and it barely mattered if they caught the Deer at all. But she was starting to feel as if the Wind-Dogs didn't understand that dogs on the ground also had to feed themselves—and their Pack—or they wouldn't be able to run at all. Every time the scent reappeared, it seemed to be coming from a different direction. The hunters would stop, scent the air, and glance at Lucky, who would not hesitate to turn them to chase after the delicious and enticing smell of the Deer, even if it meant retracing their steps.

"Should we really go *back*?" Snap gasped, as Lucky's ears swiveled and he twisted his head this way and that, trying to find the scent again after they had lost it a fourth time. She pointed with her nose. "Surely we've been going more or less in *that* direction, so the Deer must be over there. . . ."

"No, we haven't." Bruno frowned. "We've turned a circle since the beginning, remember? We haven't gone farther in any one direction than another."

"Could the Wind-Dogs just be playing with us?" Arrow wondered.

"No, there it is!" Lucky barked, and leaped into a run, without waiting for the others. His head was high and his ears were pricked up. "Follow me!"

Storm exchanged a weary glance with Arrow, but they both ran after their Beta.

We couldn't exactly let him run off alone, Storm thought. *But oh, Wind-Dogs, I hope that you come to the end of your game soon. . . . I thought I scented a whole pack of weasels in that last bush, and we must bring back something to feed the Pack. . . .*

They climbed another hill, a steep and rocky slope that had Storm wondering why the Pack couldn't have picked somewhere a bit flatter to settle, and when they got to the top, Storm looked down the other side and saw . . .

Nothing. No Golden Deer shimmering in front of them, not even the slightest glint of it on the horizon.

But she realized, as she panted harder and caught her breath, that she could *scent* something. It wasn't quite the same as the Golden Deer's scent, though there was something similar about it—this was a real, warm, living creature's scent. It didn't make her want to run and run, but it did make her start to drool.

Lucky was standing still, for the moment, scenting the air and trying to catch the strange and spicy scent of the Golden Deer again, so Storm turned away from him, following the delicious smell of prey. She rounded a large rock and looked down a steep hill that was studded with bushes and small trees, and through the cover she could see . . .

Deer! Real deer!

There were so many of them—at least four females, their soft necks curved down to nibble on the thick green grass at the bottom of the slope.

Storm looked over her shoulder and found that Arrow, Snap, and Breeze had followed her to the top of the slope, and they had seen the deer too.

"We would only need to catch one for the Pack to eat better tonight than they have in days," Breeze murmured, her eyes bright.

"With cover like this, and the wind in our favor, we could catch two, no problem," said Snap.

"We could split into pairs," said Arrow. "We're all big enough to take down a deer between two—or fast enough," he conceded, as Snap turned her head to glare up at him. "If we fan out, and all attack at once . . ."

"What are you doing?" Lucky asked. "We're already on a hunt. We can't stop now, we're so close! The Golden Deer is nearby, I'm certain of it!"

Storm glanced at the others, and she could see them all thinking the same thing—*is he actually going to ask us to leave behind a hunt like this to chase a deer that might not even be real?* But to her dismay, none of them seemed to be about to say anything.

She thought back to her dream, to Whisper saying she would fight for the dogs even if she was the only one, and sighed. *I suppose it's up to me to be the one Lucky is angry with. Again.* Still, she dipped her head as respectfully as she could and said, "Beta, the Pack needs food. The Golden Deer might bring us good luck, but it won't fill our bellies!"

"Storm's right," said Snap, and the others nodded and woofed their agreement too. "Just look at them, Beta—there are four deer down there, and we're certain we can take at least two!"

"Wouldn't it be nice to go back to Alpha with some good news, for once?" Breeze said softly.

Lucky hesitated, and while he was thinking, another gust of wind blew through the trees and bushes and washed over the dogs. Storm's mouth watered even more, and a thought struck her.

"Beta, what if this *is* the deer we're meant to find? What if the

Wind-Dogs have led us to this spot not to catch the Golden Deer, but so that we'll be in exactly the right place to hunt these real deer and feed our Pack?"

Lucky's eyes brightened. "Storm, I think you might be right! Yes, that must be it. We will hunt these deer."

Storm suppressed a bark of joy, afraid of spooking the prey— but she couldn't resist turning on the spot and wagging her tail. Lucky had made the right choice!

And who knows, perhaps the Wind-Dogs really did mean this all along. . . .

Arrow quickly relayed his idea for a plan of attack, and Lucky approved it. He and Storm would take the left-most deer, Arrow and Snap would take the right, and Bruno and Breeze would go right down the middle.

The wind stayed firmly in the same direction, blowing the deer's scents toward the dogs, but never carrying any hint of the dogs back to their prey as they crept down the slope. Storm moved stealthily between the twigs of a low bush dotted with bright-yellow flowers, as beside her Lucky stepped over a pile of crunchy-looking leaves. The others were being so quiet, she could barely tell they were there at all, except as faint moving shadows between the trees and the bushes.

They reached the bottom of the slope and slunk forward on

their bellies, getting as close as they could to the deer without spooking them. Storm put out a paw to go a little farther, but Lucky shot her a warning look, and she followed his instruction and froze where she was. Sure enough, one of the deer glanced in their direction, then shuffled around to another clump of grass and bent her head again.

Lucky glanced at Storm, and she signaled her readiness with a flick of her ears, afraid to move another muscle.

"Ready . . . *now*," hissed Lucky, and almost as one dog they stalked out from their hiding place, trying to move quietly but quickly through the tall grass, low to the ground but ready to leap. A soft rustling told Storm that the other dogs had made their moves too.

Suddenly the deer Storm was stalking looked around. Storm didn't wait to find out if it had seen her. She leaped, using every ounce of power stored up in her tense hind legs to cover the last few yards and sink her teeth into the leg of the deer. The deer gave a loud, honking roar and tried to run, but Storm closed her jaws and would not let go, and in a bright blur of golden fur Lucky leaped past her, striking the deer's side and bearing it to the ground. The deer's legs kicked out, almost throwing Storm off, and she narrowly avoided being struck in the head by a hoof. Then Lucky's teeth flashed and he bent his head to the deer's throat. There was a gurgling sound, and the deer went silent, its legs suddenly still.

Storm unlocked her jaws and stood back, panting.

"We got one!" she gasped.

There was a crashing sound as one of the deer sprinted away, slipped between two trees, and was gone, and a pounding chorus of hoofbeats as another took off at a frantic pace, bleeding from a scratch on its flank but easily outpacing Bruno and Breeze.

That left one more. Storm sat up on her hind legs to see that Arrow and Snap were still on the deer, but it was kicking and thrashing, and they were having trouble keeping it down.

"Bruno! Help Arrow!" Storm barked, and Bruno skidded around, giving up his pursuit and streaking back across the grass just in time to leap on the deer as it managed to throw Snap off with a toss of its long neck. The extra weight of Bruno, and then Breeze, was too much for the deer. It let out a last roaring cry and then sank back into the grass, where Arrow delivered the killing bite as swiftly and efficiently as Lucky had.

Lucky let out a howl of triumph. "Good work, hunters! The Pack will eat well tonight!"

CHAPTER TWENTY-ONE

It was a good thing they hadn't caught the third deer, Storm thought. The Wind-Dogs might have led them to a feast, but they'd traveled a long way from the camp, and it had taken the strength of all six dogs to drag their prey home across the fields and through the trees. They'd worked in shifts, so each dog had been able to rest for part of the way, but Storm's neck, back, and legs still ached by the time they had returned to camp.

It was a good ache, though, and it felt even better when she finally dropped her deer leg and stepped back. The prey pile might have had only two creatures in it, but it suddenly looked like a mountain of food.

The other dogs were gathering around, barking and howling in delight at the sight of the two deer and yapping congratulations to the hunters. Thorn and Beetle hopped with excitement, bouncing off each other in their eagerness to get close to the deer, and Sunshine spun around in hectic circles.

Alpha came out of her den, the four pups trailing in her wake—Nibble and Fluff in front, yipping to each other, and Tumble and Tiny following a little more slowly, their jaws wide open as they smelled the delicious prey-scent.

"There will be more than enough for every dog to eat tonight," Alpha said, fixing her large eyes on Lucky. "Thank you."

Storm watched Tumble carefully, but although he wasn't quite as fast as his litter-sisters, there was no sign of pain in his face and he wasn't limping.

The rest of the Pack drifted away from the deer as the pups came closer, the dogs all gathering around Alpha.

"I'm pleased to say that Tumble is feeling much better," she said, a hint of knowing amusement in her voice. "All four of the pups are doing very well—but they can tell you that themselves. Can't you, pups?"

She nudged Nibble forward, and Nibble looked up into the faces of the older dogs and drew herself up as big as she could.

"Fa!" she yapped. "Nib!" And with that, she bounced over to

Lucky and started trying to climb up his coat. He gave a gruff bark of laughter and obediently crouched down so that she could reach his shoulders.

"Ma? Maaaa . . ." Fluff was pawing at Alpha's leg.

"What is it, Fluff?"

Fluff drew in a huge sniff of air and then gave a high-pitched bark.

"Yes, Fluff, that's our dinner," said Alpha indulgently.

Tumble and Tiny had caught up now, and Tiny had left her litter-brother to catch his breath at Alpha's paws. She was still noticeably smaller than her litter-siblings, but Storm was rather pleased to see that what she had witnessed when she thought Wiggle was playing with the pups hadn't all been a hallucination—Tiny really could move quickly when she chose to, crawling in and out of the dogs' legs, pouncing on their wagging tails, then lying down to catch her breath.

Storm couldn't help wondering why the pups were so hypnotic to watch—they were clumsy and small, always falling over one another, making unintelligible yapping noises—but she had to admit that just like the rest of the Pack, she found it hard to look away. She couldn't help feeling soft and warm inside when she saw that Tumble's leg had gotten better, or that Tiny had grown stronger. Soon enough, they would be grown-up dogs who would have to face the bad times as well as the good. But for now, they could simply be pups, and that was strangely reassuring.

"Storm," Daisy said, tearing her attention from the pups, "will you tell us about the hunt? You were away a long time. Where did you go? How did you manage to catch two deer?"

"It wasn't that hard, actually," Storm said, and looked at Lucky, expecting him to take up the story. But he just looked back and gave her a slow blink of happiness.

"Go on, Storm, tell us what happened!" Thorn barked.

"Well," Storm said, sitting down and scratching behind one ear with her back paw, "it was strange. When we first set out, it was as if the Wind-Dogs had vanished . . . there were no scents or sounds of prey anywhere!"

A few of the other dogs turned away from the pups and faced Storm as she went on, and even Snap and Arrow sat listening, despite the fact that she was sure they could tell the story much better than she could.

"And then what happened?" Daisy prompted, as Storm paused to remember just how the second deer had been taken down.

"Bruno helped hold down the deer, and Arrow put in the final bite," said Lucky. "And I would like a word with Storm before the prey-sharing—if you don't mind, Daisy."

"Oh, but I wanted to—oh, I mean . . . yes, Beta," Daisy corrected herself quickly. Storm was glad to see that Lucky didn't seem angry. He nudged the little white-and-brown dog affectionately as he passed.

"Storm, will you come with me?"

"Of course, Beta," said Storm, and got up and followed Lucky. He led her over to the spot where the cage had been built to keep Fox Mist, and for a horrible moment she thought that he had found out what she'd done, and he was going to punish her, or threaten to throw her out of the Pack, or even just tell her again how disappointed he was. . . .

"Storm, I need to apologize to you," Lucky said, and Storm blinked at him in surprise. "I have treated you badly over the last few days. It's been a stressful time. I was so afraid and angry when Tumble was hurt. . . ." He hesitated, then shook himself briefly and met Storm's eyes again. "I know that it wasn't your fault. Any dog can misstep in a fight, especially a dog who hasn't been sleeping well. I'm so used to you being such a good fighter that I thought you should have been there, but that wasn't fair of me."

"Thank you, Beta," Storm said. Her heart felt full and warm, and when Lucky gave her a lick on the ear, she dipped her head to accept it. "I've been . . . troubled, recently. But I'm feeling better now. I want to help the Pack every way I can," she added, feeling buoyed up by happiness.

"Every dog, gather 'round," barked Alpha's voice. "It's time to eat this feast our brave hunters have brought home for us!"

Storm opened her jaws and panted happily, wagging her tail hard. "I can't wait, I'm so hungry!" And with that she turned and bounded across the camp, settling down between Daisy and Bella, feeling content.

Maybe I was wrong about the prey pile, she thought. *Prey does go bad. Maybe everything that's happened has just been . . . coincidence, or terrible misunderstandings. Anyone could have taken the prey Moon was blamed for eating—every dog makes mistakes, don't they? The fox cub might have been killed by some other creature and left behind near our camp.*

And Whisper . . .

He could have been killed by the coyotes after all, Storm told herself— but she felt a ripple of unease as she thought it. She tried to ignore the feeling that she was betraying something by considering the possibility—after all, the coyotes were bad creatures, and which of her Packmates could possibly be as bad as them, or worse? Eager little Daisy? Twitch, with his seemingly endless patience and wisdom? Breeze, the hero who had saved the pups and who was always so kind and thoughtful? Lucky, or even *Alpha*? Sunshine? Mickey, Rake, Bella, Arrow . . . they were *all* her Pack, and Pack meant loyalty. How could Storm accuse a single one of them, especially when none of them had even thought of accusing her? There had to be a different explanation, and whatever it was, she would find it.

Alpha and Lucky had both eaten, stripping off large chunks of deer meat without having to think about how much would be left for the lower-ranked dogs—it looked as if Sunshine would have half a deer all to herself. Twitch stepped forward next, licking his lips, and then took a big bite out of the deer's hind leg.

The whine that came from Twitch's throat was long and high, like a howl that had been caught behind his teeth. It was a howl of awful, excruciating pain. All around the camp, the dogs cringed back, their ears pressed down in fright. Tumble, Nibble, Fluff, and Tiny all hid behind Alpha, and Storm wanted to do the same.

She could smell the blood. Not the prey-scent of the deer, but dog blood, fresh and frightening.

Twitch stumbled back, choking, spitting blood. Snap and Daisy both sprang across the clearing toward him at once, with Rake not far behind them. Sunshine got to her paws, looked at the blood dripping from Twitch's jaws, and sank down to the grass in a faint. Alpha extracted herself from among the pups and hurried over, and one by one the rest of the dogs rose, sickened dismay in their faces.

"It's all right, Twitch, open your mouth. . . ." Snap said, in a cool voice that barely trembled at all. Twitch gave another strangled, gargling howl, shaking his head, suddenly unsteady on his three legs. Daisy turned an anxious circle and then reared up and pushed him. He fell hard on his side.

"I'm sorry!" Daisy yapped.

"Let me see," Snap said, and Twitch managed to open his jaws. "Oh my . . . Daisy, put your paws on his head, stop him from moving," she said. Daisy obeyed, and Mickey ran to help her. "Twitch, this might hurt. Try to hold still." Snap put her small paw inside Twitch's mouth and clawed something out. It fell onto the grass, a lump of . . . Storm couldn't see what, except that it looked like a solid and glinting drop of blood about the size of one of her claws. Twitch yelped again.

"Let Snap do this, Twitch," said Alpha, resting her paw on his shoulder, and then turning to sniff at the leg of the deer.

A horrible feeling of certainty pulled Storm forward, and she stepped around Twitch's writhing form and Snap's pawing at the inside of his mouth, to look at the deer's hind leg where he had bitten it. Arrow followed her, gazing over Storm's shoulder at the leg. A chunk of deer had been torn away, and underneath . . .

"It's *clear-stone*," Alpha gasped. "This part of the deer is full of shards of broken clear-stone!"

Storm didn't understand. Alpha couldn't mean clear-stone—the strange, sharp, see-through stuff that longpaw houses and loudcages were full of?

But as she watched Snap fish more pieces of glinting red stuff out of Twitch's mouth, she realized that Alpha was right.

"*What?*" barked Lucky. "But how could that be?"

"Maybe when you were dragging them home . . ." Moon began, but Breeze's whine cut her off.

"No, there's no way." Breeze stepped forward, her eyes wide with shock. "This is . . . it's not . . ."

"There was no clear-stone on the way here," Storm agreed, in a voice barely louder than a pup's whimper.

"The deer were fine when we put them down here," Breeze yapped. She looked around the camp, turning twice on the spot on shaking paws. Storm started toward her, thinking that she might faint or turn hysterical with panic, but instead Breeze stopped, staring hard at Twitch's bleeding mouth. "They were fine. This happened *after* we got the deer home. Do you know what that means? It means *some dog did this!*" she howled.

Storm froze, the truth of it hitting her all at once.

A dog did this. A dog stole the prey, and poisoned Bella and Daisy, and killed the fox cub, and killed Whisper.

A dog in our Pack.

She whined and dug into the ground with her paws as slowly, one by one, she saw a similar realization dawn on the rest of the Pack. Arrow's shoulder pressed against hers, and she could feel how tense he was.

Is this what I wanted? She had wished that the others would accept the truth, that they could see it as clearly as she could, but then she too had been lulled into believing that maybe it couldn't be true. Now they all knew there was a bad dog here, and they were all staring at Breeze, and then at Twitch, and then slowly they began to stare at one another.

Each one of them was imagining their Packmates sabotaging the prey, wondering which of their friends could have done this.

And then, with an ache that felt like Storm's heart shrinking in her chest, she saw dogs' heads turning toward her and Arrow, their eyes cold.

At last, they've accepted that there's a traitor here.

But they think that traitor is Arrow. Or me.

DON'T MISS

THE GATHERING DARKNESS

SURVIVORS

BOOK 3:
INTO THE SHADOWS

With Alpha and Beta's new pups underpaw, the dogs of the Wild

Pack should be celebrating and looking toward their future. But

there is a traitor in their midst, and tensions—and suspicions—

keep rising. Storm is determined to protect her Pack . . . but if they

don't find the traitor soon, there may not be a Pack left to protect.

CHAPTER ONE

How could this have happened?

Broken shards of clear-stone, Storm realized with horror, had been concealed in the very prey the Pack dogs were about to eat. Two fat, splendid deer, the finest prey pile the Pack had seen in many turns of the Moon-Dog—and some dog had sabotaged it. *Why?*

Every dog wore a look of stunned disgust. Bella, just behind Storm, whimpered with distress, but even her loyal mate—Storm's fellow Fierce Dog, Arrow—was too horrified to comfort her. He stood at Storm's shoulder, trembling with shock. Most of the Pack was silent, staring, their hackles bristling. Breeze's howl of incredulity still echoed on the air—and Storm knew how she felt.

Storm had suspected for a while that there must be some dog in the Pack who was working against them all, but even she

1

could hardly believe a member of the Pack had done this appalling thing. They had all been so happy tonight, sharing the spoils of a wonderful hunt—and now the Pack's Third Dog lay on the ground, choking and whimpering, while Snap eased the treacherous shards from his bloodied mouth. They glinted where she dropped them, cruelly sharp and wet with blood.

Daisy, holding Twitch's russet-furred head steady with her two small forepaws, licked his ear, whining wretchedly. "Please try to hold still. It's nearly done."

"Oh no, oh no. Oh, Twitch. You poor thing," Sunshine whimpered as she tried to help Daisy and Snap by moving the clear-stone away from their paws and into a small pile.

Since Breeze had let loose her howl of distress, since the Pack had finally realized there was a traitor in their midst, the other dogs had stood there, frozen, staring at one another in horror. But now, Storm felt a prickling down her spine as little Ruff turned and fixed her gaze on Arrow. There was accusation in Ruff's eyes. Storm glared at her, but even as she did so, she saw Bruno also turn and stare. One by one, the heads of all the Packmates were turning toward Arrow.

It's Arrow they don't trust. Just because he's a Fierce Dog!

But I'm a Fierce Dog, too, and I was the one who tried to warn them....

Her heart pounded in her chest with fear and with anger at the unfairness of it all. She was certain that Arrow would no more have sabotaged the prey with clear-stone than she would herself. Yet he was the first suspect that leaped to every dog's mind.

Bruno was the first to growl his thoughts aloud. The burly dog showed his sharp teeth. "I told you. I said it all along. You can't trust a Fierce Dog."

Storm's fur prickled with resentment, but he was glaring at Arrow, his snarl menacing. "I never wanted that Fierce Dog in the Pack!"

Storm's rage boiled up, smothering her fear. She hadn't slept properly in many journeys of the Sun-Dog, afraid *she* was the Bad Dog, afraid of what she might do if she walked in her sleep again. She realized now that she wasn't responsible for the terrible things that had befallen the Pack. Knowing that she had tortured herself and worried that she was a bad dog, while all the time there had been a real traitor lurking, made her even angrier. And that Bruno should assume Arrow was the traitor, just because he, like Storm, was a Fierce Dog, was worse still.

"How dare you, Bruno? Arrow's done nothing to deserve

3

that!" It felt good to release her fury at last, to lash out at the dog who made so many snide remarks about Fierce Dogs. "He's been a loyal Pack member from the start—even if you refuse to realize it!"

"Ha," growled Ruff softly. "We should have known."

Storm spun on the little black dog, her ears swiveling forward. "What do you mean? Say it out loud!"

"Gladly," sneered Ruff, the little black dog who had once been Omega in Twitch's Pack. "One Fierce Dog stands up for the other one. What a surprise."

Before Storm could snap back, Dart too gave a low snarl. "You don't have to stand up for Arrow, Storm. He isn't like you—it's not like he's been one of us for long. You've proven yourself to this Pack. What do we know about him? *Nothing.*"

"Nothing," added Chase, "except that he betrayed his last Pack. Didn't he?"

"Wait just a minute!" Bella sprang forward, her golden hackles raised. "Arrow betrayed the Fierce Dogs to save all of us! You've got no reason to blame him. And he couldn't have sabotaged the prey—I know it! I've been with him the whole time, ever since the hunters brought it back to camp."

"Oh yes?" Tall, scruffy Rake cocked his head, eyes narrowing.

"You never took your eyes off him, then? You weren't distracted, even for a moment?"

"Every dog gets distracted," growled Woody. "Especially with Alpha's new pups around. You can't have watched Arrow *all* the time, Bella."

"Well, I did," she snapped defiantly. "I always know where Arrow is. *Always!*"

"Huh," sneered Ruff, shaking her head. "Is that so? Why's that, Bella?"

Ruff has a lot more to say than usual, thought Storm bitterly, *now that she's attacking Fierce Dogs.*

"I want to know that, too." Dart curled her thin muzzle, eyeing Bella keenly. "What makes you so aware of Arrow all of a sudden, Bella? Is there something you need to tell us?"

Bella paused for a moment, lifting her head, and Storm saw a muscle in her throat jerk. Her own heart was in her mouth, because she alone knew what was coming. Was Bella going to admit the truth now? It would be harder than ever, at this moment, to make the Pack accept it.

The golden dog's hackles were still lifted as she curled back her muzzle. "Yes," Bella told them defiantly. "Arrow and I are mates. We have been for some time."

For a long moment there was silence, except for the pained whimpering of Twitch as Snap stepped back from him, her awful job finally done.

Then Breeze spoke for the first time since she'd howled in horror. Her voice was uncertain but clear in the quiet camp.

"But in that case . . . Alpha?" She turned to their slender leader, the swift-dog. "I'm sorry, but we *can't* take Bella's word for it, can we? If she's Arrow's mate, she's bound to defend him."

"No!" Lucky, the Pack's golden-furred Beta, barked loudly. "I know Bella better than any of you"—though Storm noticed he shot a suddenly doubtful look at Arrow, as if to say *maybe not as well as I thought*—"and she would never be with a dog who would turn on his own Pack. If Arrow was a bad dog, my litter-sister wouldn't be his mate." With a glance at Bella, he paused to catch his breath, shook himself a little, and licked his chops uncertainly. Whatever he said, Lucky couldn't hide his surprise at Bella's announcement.

Well, Storm told herself, *it was a shocking way to find out.* No doubt Bella had hoped to choose a better moment to break the news to her litter-brother, a far higher-ranking dog.

"I'm not so sure." That was Dart, who sat back on her brown-and-white haunches, tapping her tail thoughtfully. There was a spiteful gleam in her eye. "It wouldn't be the first time Bella's chosen unsavory allies."

Mickey, the kind old black-and-white Farm Dog, gave an angry growl. "That's in the past, Dart. Don't drag it up again like rotten prey."

Storm shifted uneasily. She knew what they were talking about: the time Bella had allied herself with a mob of foxes to try to force the Pack's half wolf former Alpha to share their territory. It had been a reckless strategy, one that backfired horribly, as Bella herself had told Storm.

But this was no time for Dart to bring that up! It was just another vindictive, painful dig at Bella, who was truly remorseful about her foolishness. And it was another way of getting at Arrow. Storm felt her lip curling.

All the dogs had turned to Alpha now, waiting for her answer to Breeze. The gray swift-dog looked very thoughtful, but she hadn't so much as growled.

"Well, Alpha?" Bruno nodded at Breeze, then looked directly back at his leader. "Do you agree with our Beta, or with Breeze? Are you going to rely on Bella's word, given that she's the Fierce Dog's mate now?"

Storm suppressed a gasp of shock. Such open defiance of

their Beta—she'd known Bruno wasn't fond of Arrow, but surely Alpha would slap down the burly Fight Dog now? Anger roiled in Storm's gut, but she was too confused and hot with fury to say any more. *It's up to Alpha now, to make these dogs see how ridiculous their accusations are!*

Alpha swung her narrow head, gazing around the clearing at each dog in turn. Her expression was a combination of disappointment and irritation, but her growl was cool. "It's too soon to point a paw at any dog. Every dog here needs to calm down and stop grabbing at dry bones." She nodded at Twitch, who lay exhausted with pain, his flanks heaving. "Twitch has been hurt. This is not the time for destructive quarrels!"

"But, Alpha!" barked Bruno.

"We've got to put a stop to this right now," whined Woody, "and Arrow's the most likely culprit!"

"It's obvious, isn't it?" growled Dart sulkily.

"That is enough." Alpha's snarl was deadly. She said no more, only stared into their eyes until every dog coughed and muttered, then fell into shamefaced silence. Nor did the swift-dog spare Storm; she glared into her eyes with a directness that brooked no further argument. Storm clenched her jaws and resisted the urge to howl at the injustice.

ERIN
HUNTER

is inspired by a fascination with
the ferocity of the natural world.
As well as having great respect for
nature in all its forms, Erin enjoys
creating rich, mythical explanations
for animal behavior. She is also the
author of the bestselling Warriors,
Seekers, and Bravelands series.

Visit the Packs online at
www.survivorsdogs.com!

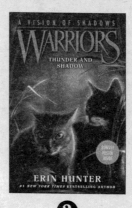

WARRIORS: THE NEW PROPHECY

1

2

3

4

5

6

In the second series, follow the next generation of heroic cats as they set off on a quest to save the Clans from destruction.

HARPER
An Imprint of HarperCollins *Publishers*

WARRIORS : POWER OF THREE

1   **2**   **3**

4   **5**   **6**

In the third series, Firestar's grandchildren begin their training as warrior cats. Prophecy foretells that they will hold more power than any cats before them.

HARPER
An Imprint of HarperCollinsPublishers

WARRIORS: OMEN OF THE STARS

1

2

3

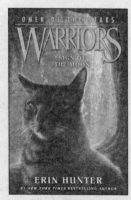

4

5

6

In the fourth series, find out which ThunderClan
apprentice will complete the prophecy.

HARPER
An Imprint of HarperCollinsPublishers

www.warriorcats.com